PRAISE FOR BONES OF STARLIGHT & EVA L. ELASIGUE

Writers of the Future 31 Contest Finalist
for excerpt from Fire Within

"We were thrilled..."
- Seattle Review of Books

"A uniquely told and intertwining story, evoking interstellar mystery and a
deadly inheritance, all brimming with artistic vibrancy."
- Josh Vogt, author of The Cleaners series & Forge of Ashes

"I enjoyed it thoroughly."
- Margaret Bumby, attendee at World Science Fiction & Fantasy Convention 75 Helsinki

"Eva Elasigue's debut novel, Bones of Starlight: Fire on all Sides, is a
pan-galactic sci-fi told in lyrical passages that keep the pages turning. The
world building develops naturally as the story unfolds and events happen
all over the galaxy, with a fantastic host of players from a variety of races
and worlds. A stupendous opening to a new space operatic series."
- Vanessa MacLellan, author of Three Great Lies

"She makes the act of envisioning a universe, giving it life on paper, and
making it accessible to her readers seem like a simple feat. Though her
writing charmed me with its luminous quality, much like Le Guin's, Ms.
Elasigue has her own voice. It is miraculous and full of warmth, and one
to cherish."
- Zeta Moore, of Alfie Award-winning periodical Black Gate

"I really enjoyed it!"
- Daniel Sloan, circus & performance artist

"It's really good."
- Richard Chwedyk, Nebula Award-winning author of Bronte's Egg

"By the time I was a few chapters in, I had a difficult time putting this book down. It reminds me of the science fiction I used to read as a teen-ager, such as Anne McCaffrey's series Dragonriders of Pern, stories rich in lore and inventive history. I thought this book was merely going to be about space-age intrigue - not quite my style - but I was very pleasantly surprised by the intricate story that drew me in. The author deftly weaves different viewpoints and experiences together from several characters - you're never sure where the story might lead you next, but you can't wait to find out. I will be waiting impatiently to get my hands on the next book of this series!"
- J.R., Amazon reviewer

"Great Story. Strong characters. Interesting plot. Effective writing style in which the tech and politics flow smoothly - reminds me of Herbert. Looking forward to next in series! Keep an eye on this author."
- Sandsage, Amazon reviewer

"Amazing read! The expert weaving of a an intricate future civilization with a story that rivals the likes of Dune in scope and imagery. A masterful first novel that challenges the imagination to keep up with it! Can't wait to read the sequel!"
- DaVinci's Shadow, Amazon reviewer

"Fantastic"
- Isaac Cotec, Subaqueous music

"Captures the magick."
- Musickcasting, selection broadcaster

"We're all just characters in one of [Elasigue's] stories."
- Robert Kyte, sometime Mississippi radio jockey and Friday Harbor dock agent schmoperator

"One helluva writer."
- Alex Murphy, sci-fi horror movie fan

This title is available on Amazon Kindle.

<u>Also by the Author</u>

various poetry
including illustrated handwritten copier broadsheet "The Process"

The Realization of Self-Identity, or: Beevenge
a short story hosted online by Breathe Publication/Medium

Inventors of the Invisible World
a stage monologue performed at Friday Harbor Fringefest 2014

articles on McSweeney's Internet Tendency:
Chocolate-Covered Sunflower Seeds
Peanut Brittle Cheesecake
"Inner Meet Me" by The Beta Band

BONES OF STARLIGHT

1

fire within

by

EVA L. ELASIGUE

PRIMAL SPIRAL

This is a work of fiction. Names, characters, places and incidents are either from the author's imagination or are used fictitiously, and any resemblance to actual persons, living or dead, business establishments, events or locales in our physically occupied universe is entirely coincidental.

released serially online at bonesofstarlight.com
jacket art: "Golden Compass" painting by Leo Shallat
decorative fonts by gLuk
jacket design by Primal Spiral

websites:
bonesofstarlight.com
evalisaelasigue.wordpress.com

Hardcover Re-Issue, 1st printing
ISBN: 978-1-944416-11-9
previously published as Bones of Starlight: Fire On All Sides
via Primal Spiral, 685 Spring Street #254, Friday Harbor WA 98250
primal.spiral@gmail.com

To V
without whom

CONTENTS

1ST SEQUENCE

Coffee Mug / 1
Your Eminence / 2
Market Districts / 3
Full Regalia / 4
Easy Breezy / 5
Between Courtesies / 6
Monument / 7
Synchronize
Huntresses' Aria / 8
Petite Disarmingly / 9
Shadow Forest / 10
Hook Slider / 11
Moon Moth / 12
These Stars / 13

2ND SEQUENCE

Com Relay / 14
Elongated Runnerbird / 15
Skeleton Crew / 16
Morning Rocketeers / 17
Uh Expertise / 18
Aces Too / 19
Access Stairways / 20
Secret Nowhere / 21

3RD SEQUENCE

22 \ Magma Veins
23 \ Theta Rhythms
24 \ Surrounding Forces
25 \ Powder Apples
26 \ Mother's Milk
27 \ Emotional Voices
28 \ Two Honklizards
29 \ Unreachable Slumber
30 \ Disaster Signal
31 \ Well Guarded
32 \ Fiery Assembly
33 \ Surface Expressions
34 \ Concentric Platters
35 \ Central Beacon

4TH SEQUENCE

36 \ Different Kinds
37 \ Blood Debt
38 \ Planetwide Network
39 \ Scrutinizing Unimpressed
40 \ Hover Life
41 \ Further Transformations
42 \ Display Brightened

5th sequence

Shimmering Heat / 43
Planet Sunrise / 44
Rhythmic / 45
Connection
Typically Austere / 46
Refugee Belongings / 47
Classroom / 48
Broadcast
Autonomous / 49
Network
Spreading Leaves / 50
Bootsteps / 51
Approached
False Echoes / 52
Their Rendezvous / 53
Long Hunt / 54
Grave Injustice / 55
Poison Evident / 56
Skip Town / 57
Spacefaring Voices / 58
Engines Entropy / 59

6th sequence

Intrepid Backup / 60
Completely / 61
Uneventful
Sakhana & Zoe / 62
Pyrean Vision / 63
Traffic Signals / 64
Disruption Patterns / 65
Appointed Route / 66
Thunderous Hearing / 67

7th sequence

68 \ Vine Curtain
69 \ First Sweep
70 \ Priority Observations
71 \ First Sweep
72 \ Help Themselves
73 \ Hard Gazes
74 \ Past Decisions

8th sequence

75 \ Unusual Problem
76 \ Farewell Letter
77 \ Fully Understandable
78 \ Painful Attempts
79 \ Glow Remaining
80 \ Outer Orbit

9th sequence

81 \ Something Nebulous
82 \ Possible Avenue
83 \ Surprise Finding
84 \ Office Working
85 \ Full Qualifications
86 \ Anomalous Environment
87 \ Arcane Nature
88 \ Rolling Ballad

+ Re-Issue Details
+ Grammatical Notes
+ Thanks

BONES OF STARLIGHT:

Fire Within

1st
sequence

1

In the cold hour before dawn, the shipping dock workers were wiping their noses and shouting, filling the blackness with sound and business. Derringer stood in a nearby alley, one hand with a smoke, the other cradling his forehead. Everything was still too loud, though he'd recovered somewhat from a couple hours ago when his client's case had come to call. He broke up the fight by giving the intruder a solid one to the head with a coffee mug, which was worth the rest of his fee. It was just as well.

Another ship arrived a block over. Derringer held his coat over his face, shutting his eyes against the dust billowing past him. The ship dropped a few feet onto its landing gear, the hull hitting the ground with a loud scrape. Their suspension was shot.

He finished his smoke and turned away from the dock, on a meandering path through the warehouses. A few had their lights on, but most were shut down. Derringer knew what went on behind some of those doors; the sheer volume of things he knew kept him moving. Being a decent private investigator means that eventually, people learn his face. He did his best to keep his image out of pictures and papers, but in some cases it just can't be helped. He knew when it was time to leave a city – or a planet. He was never the only one watching.

It was his first time back on Alisandre in four years, and he was free, for now. Time to take a look around, see what had become of the place. The buildings of Alisandre Capital spiraled and curved, thrust and shone against a clear sky.

The morning brightened as Derringer turned toward his rented flat. He could see the Aquarii were busy here with their art. Colors shifted and swirled on the walls, blues and greys echoing the streets' calm. The colors and shapes echoed the outermost level of thought, so if you had anything to hide, you'd better be good at hiding it in this neighborhood. Derringer had long ago learned how to manipulate that, like the diplomats and councillors.

Ahead of him a door opened, a small red-haired woman hurrying out of it carrying a basket. The doorway swirled purple and black around her, tendrils of color following as she hummed the tune of an old-time march. She had the look of a Capital woman, eyes forever creased in a facsimile of good intentions, lips shut tight holding back her words. As she passed him, the wall swirled magenta. Oh ho, thought Derringer. She thinks I'm handsome.

} 2 {

"How are you feeling today, Your Eminence?"

"All things considered, not bad." The old woman smiled over her glasses from behind the desk. "How are you today, Dr. Basa?"

"I am well, Your Eminence. Thank you for asking."

"Glad to hear it. Let's get on with this then, I'm ready to bleed." Her smile showed a trace of irony as she rose and walked out from behind her desk, past her bodyguards to the pair of chairs near the door. Her heeled shoes set her some inches above the doctor, for she was tall, and her grey coif only increased her stature. The legs showing beneath the yellow knee-length suit skirt were still shapely, though she walked slowly; a floor-length russet cape whispered trailing behind her, the velvet shimmering. Placing a hand on the chair arm, she sat gracefully, though not without tension. She gestured to the chair facing her, holding the doctor's gaze with dark brown eyes.

Dr. Basa sat, placing his kit on the floor. The acting leader of the Pan-Galactic Imperium, 24th in the Magus dynasty, pulled her collar to one side. With a large metal stylus, the doctor pricked her at the crook of her neck; the inside of her right elbow; and at her left ankle. The two kept their silence during the sample analysis. The Queen turned her head to the window view: a bright, warm day with vehicles of council and court weaving about the imperial grounds. Beyond that, the towers and neighborhoods of Alisandre Capital, themselves dispersing into the contours of the mountain's slopes.

The device beeped. The doctor read the results silently, taking the time to read them again. "It's... much as expected, Your Eminence. The tests show your condition continues to worsen." They shared a moment of consolation. "How is your appetite?"

"Well, you know I can't eat like I used to. But I still can, so there is that."

"Have you felt any shortness of breath?"

"My limbs are weak. I can't do much, and I need a lot of rest. But it's just how things are – nothing seems to have changed from yesterday or the day before."

"No, you wouldn't necessarily feel it so dramatically."

From the chair where she waited in the hallway, Soleil could hear the ruffled murmur of question and answer. Though she couldn't make out the words, her grandmother's tone was bemused, if impatient with the familiar protocol. Soleil hummed a tune under her breath, a village cooking fire song.

The voices grew intelligible as they drew closer to the door. "Thank you, Dr. Basa. Give my warm regards to your wife and children."

"I will, Your Eminence. As always, it is my greatest honor to serve you and the Pan-Galactic Imperium." Soleil stood as the door opened. "Madam Princess, good to see you."

"Doctor, thank you for all you do for us. Be well." They bowed, and as he left, the guards opened the door for Soleil to enter. She walked in and dropped her most formal curtsey, head bowed though smiling. "Your Eminence."

Celeste, Magus the 24th, walked to her granddaughter and put a gentle hand under her chin. "Soleil. Rise. And give me a hug." The girl rose, and ignoring their formal dress, they gave each other a long squeeze. "That's more like it," said the old woman through closed eyes.

Letting go, the Queen looked to her guards. "Leave us. But," she said as the four filed to the door, "please send someone with refreshments. Hot tea."

"Yes, Your Eminence." The last in line nodded and closed the door behind him.

"Let's sit by the window." The two women, one old and grand, one young and fresh, walked over to the two armchairs bathed in sunlight. They sat, both arranging their finery. Celeste gazed over at her granddaughter. "Time in the countryside has done you good. Rosy cheeks, new dress, hairstyle – I love it."

"You like the dress?" Soleil beamed, smoothing her hands over the weave bearing Inka leaves and scenes of rolling hills. "The textiles of Darye are truly impressive. This dress was made by Sujen, one of the great tailors there, during the week I stayed. It was an honor." Soleil smiled as she gazed into the distance.

"Mm. Yes." A pensive look crossed the face of the old Queen.

"And you, grandmaria... well?" Soleil asked pointedly, using the old family nickname. "I did worry." She studied the elder woman, looking for any shake in her limbs, pallor to her skin.

The Queen nodded. "I am well, thank you Soleil. As well as ever I am. Certainly not as well as you. But my body is still strong, even if I need more rest than I used to. Anyone my age can say the same, I'm very fortunate to be doing as well as I am. The doctor does his tests, and they show better or worse... still, after six years of better or worse, what they say means very little to me. All I have to say is this old tower isn't toppling any time soon." She winked.

A knock sounded on the door. "Refreshments, for your Graces."

"Yes, enter," spoke Celeste. Through the door came a woman pushing a wheeled cart bearing a tea service and covered platter. The Queen gestured to the space between herself and her granddaughter. "Set it here, thank you."

The woman pushed the cart there and uncovered the platter, revealing an assortment of light food. She filled their cups, setting everything in its place till it was arranged to her satisfaction. She bowed and left.

Soleil leaned over to inspect the offerings. Her eyes landed on small bowls filled with a mass of noodle-like shiny green tendrils. "Is this seaweed?"

Celeste took her cup of tea between her hands, inhaling the rising steam. "Yes it is dear, from Foshan."

"Oooh." Soleil picked a bowl and a pair of chopsticks from the cart and took a nibble. "Mmmm." She swallowed and sighed.

"What can you tell me about Foshan?"

These pop quizzes were a tradition, and Soleil was ready. "The majority of its surface is covered by oceans, with a scattering of small, isolated islands. It was the eighth planet to join the Imperium, during the reign of Arnelle, Magus

the 6th. Acquisition was peaceful, as it was inhabited only by
a small number of Dragons, who had brought the planet to
our attention. Today, Foshan's islands support small human
and Aquariid populations. It's one of the four planets whose
solstice falls on Pyrean Midsummer." She brought another
bite of seaweed to her mouth and chewed.

Celeste nodded, smiling. "Name some exports."

"These include cordage, nets, fluid chemicals used in the
production of fuel, and," she gestured with her chopsticks,
"seaweed."

"Very good." Celeste sipped her tea. They watched a
group of vehicles navigate to the council administration,
small pods arcing in formation along an invisible airway. "You
visited all the Skandarian villages by land, I hear?"

The girl nodded. "We traveled in carts pulled by oxen.
A first for me, and somewhat less comfortable than a flier.
Though there is a charm to it. It's how nearly all the villagers
travel, if not by foot."

"How were the roads?"

Soleil's eyebrows twitched up at the question. "Roads...
were more like cart trails." A small laugh escaped.
"Occasionally they were paved, but then you would almost
wish they weren't. I don't think they have any way to maintain
pavement – the dirt road sections were actually somewhat

smoother. It was long hours traveling, grandmaria. Except when local riders would accompany us. They have loud voices, and good stories. They like to sing."

"Well, I'm glad they kept you entertained." Picking chopsticks from the cart, the Queen took a dumpling off its plate. "Tell me what you saw in the towns."

"We made a loop, Arkahn to Starhn to Darius to Darye. There aren't a lot of people left in Arkahn and Starhn, at least it seemed that way to me. Maybe everyone was in the hills with their flocks? What I saw was rather desolate. In Darius the fiber harvests have been poor, and they say the past two years have brought unhappy weather. They can't produce much, and families there have been on meager rations. But spirits are still high, and they asked but didn't beg for food assistance. Darye is prosperous with the textile trade – it's actually a fairly sizable town, which makes me think maybe that's where the young people of Arkahn and Starhn have gone." They continued their talk until the sun began to set.

} 3 {

There were five major market districts in Capital city. There was the Array, a boulevard lined with trees and shops where people would walk with their tiny pets - scalebirds, suede-skinned decapeds, anything small, exotic and expensive. At Green Hills, people could get common goods, anything they desired, at decent price and quality.

Another of these markets was Division, and it was here Derringer found himself wearing his formals. Division was a selective market on Sundays. It wasn't at all like bustling Saturdays, or the chaos of street-wide freight Tuesdays. Today, Division was practically deserted. There would be the occasional solitary person outside a closed establishment. As a general rule, they were well-dressed, with refined but understated tailoring, and you never could quite meet their eyes unless they were looking for you.

Derringer carried a medium leather satchel at his side, half full of lumpy objects. He stopped at a gated facade and rang the buzzer. At the obnoxious sound, Derringer opened the gate, heading up the front steps, and in.

The ground level of the house was a pastiche of rare and aged objects, some of them ancient. Though the place felt crowded, there was a sense that this multitude of objects had been arranged so the eye would rest on each in turn.

The detective walked up a narrow flight of stairs, toward a noise that grew louder the closer he approached. It was rhythmic, though not consistent – short outbursts of unrelated beats, each expressing a capsule of thought, a staccato statement.

Through the near left door of the narrow hallway, a lean man with wild hair was juggling five or six balls of different color and size. Occasionally he would send them flying toward glowing color patches on the walls, which would change and move when hit. It was that sound, the percussion of orb against house, that was making that unpredictable music.

Derringer watched as some rearrangements were made, having no real idea what they signified. The different orbs, he knew, were Jacobs' own modified phronium housings, so there must be some elemental interaction with the color and spacing. One by one the balls slowly came to rest in the orchestrator's arms. He then chucked them rapid-fire into a bag hanging in the corner. While the last one was in the air, he turned and grinned.

"D my man," he said, throwing open his arms. He stripped off his perspiration-soaked undershirt and threw it at the wall, revealing a collection of mandala tattoos spread across his chest. "If you're here it means you've found me some precious metals." He walked over and clapped a hand on Derringer's shoulder.

Derringer lifted the bag in his right hand. "Also brought you some essential vitamins and minerals."

He brought his other hand to Derringer's other shoulder and squeezed them both. "And this is why, we are friends to the end." He led the detective back down the stairs and down another hallway. The house went a lot deeper than it looked from the front. "Got a minute? I'm going to freshen up. Meet you in the red room." He disappeared into a bathroom, the door slamming shut.

Derringer strolled on down, ducking through a doorway on the right with a sheet pinned over it. The room was small, containing little but for a folding table and a set of chairs. On the table were scattered some small scientific instruments, and above that dominating the room was a lamp the size of a double sink hanging from the ceiling. It emitted a visible red-violet wavelength, and was the only source of light in the room.

He pulled up two chairs and sat. Humming softly, he reached into his bag and began arranging the objects on the table. There were five metal balls, all of them smaller than a fist. Through the small window in the top of each came a soft glow, its unique shade visible under the lamplight. Derringer respectfully passed his hand behind them, seeing the colors light up his palm. In the magenta light, his own skin looked bruised.

The sound of boots approached down the hall. The sheet flicked aside to reveal mathematician-coder Casper Jacobs, looking ready to party all night. Black pants covered in silver studs, black mesh tank top, leather gloves and boots. On his head sat a black Peter Pan hat sporting a pheasant feather. He beheld the objects on the table and rushed toward them, hands ready to worship.

Derringer reached into his bag and pulled out one more, bigger object. Aloft he held a softball-sized black lump with lumps on it. "Aquariid charcoal truffle."

Casper Jacobs whirled to face him with a howl of delight. He released a sigh of desire as his hands closed around the lump. He brought it to eye level, turning it this way and that. "This specimen," he said, "is a paragon of its type. This should be on display. And thanks to you, you gorgeous gumshoe, it's mine." He set it down with infinite care on the table and left the room.

He returned almost immediately with a red silk cloth, which he wrapped around the truffle, using the ends to tie the parcel to his belt. He leaned forward in his chair and looked Derringer in the eye. "Your timing is good."

Soleil sat while two women made a production of her long, black hair. She could see her reflection in a mirror surrounded by soft, tiny lightbulbs. She wore a champagne silk dressing gown with woven patterns of her family's crest.

They manipulated her hair in architectural folds and rolls, affixing it with precious ornaments. The centerpiece of their creations was a large metal hairpiece bearing a charged ruby, emanating a low glow.

She withstood the assault first of her hairdressers, her costumers, then her makeup artists, and her jewelers. Before long, she stood at the same mirror, in full regalia, alone. She stood still, conserving her energy.

The doorknob on the second door in the room clicked, the one leading from the antechamber where visitors could wait. In came a girl with bright red hair, shorter than the Princess, but with the same build and alabaster skin showing their link as cousins. "Margeaux," said Soleil, turning on her heels, "you're here. Thank goodness. I can't do these press dinners without you."

"I don't know why that would be. It's not me they come to see." She carefully placed her hands on Soleil's arms where the sleeves wouldn't wrinkle and gave them a squeeze. "It's good to have you around after your countryside tour."

Margeaux held onto her cousin, scrutinizing her. "I'm a little surprised you're dressed in capital colors."

Soleil turned her head to see herself in the mirror. The black, white, red and gold stood out in brazen geometry. "Well, strength and solidarity of the royal family, you know. I've been gone, now I'm back; and instead of seeing a princess errant in provincial clothes, they see the scion of Magus." She tilted up the corner of her lip. "More or less."

"Oh, I'd say it's a sufficient glamour. As always." Margeaux assumed a grave and official air as she faced the Scion Princess and gave a deep courtesy, the first of what would be many. Soleil returned the gesture with her most elaborate bow. All her baubles and folds of material stayed properly pinned, and the girls smiled.

The cameras began recording when the great doors opened into Troyen's Reception Hall. Magus Scion Princess Soleil entered at the head of a retinue, all dressed in the colors of the royal seat at Alisandre Capital. In her left hand she carried an eagle statue, and in her right was an orb of stone, as dark as deep space with flashes of aurora green and blue.

She stopped before her two parents, King and Queen Ascendant. The retinue broke into a new formation, that let each person in the party witness the royal reception with their own eyes.

A calculated dancelike flourish, Princess Soleil executed the body language that described deepest respect, and offered the two objects before her. Her mother picked up the globe of stone, and her father the eagle.

Margeaux was not anywhere near the front of the retinue, but from her distance she could still see everything. The hall must have been chosen for its size to accommodate the formal arrangement. Large, but nowhere as large as the minor amphitheater. Her mind wandered during the series of gestures to the Queen Regent, who stood imposing in a long gown of red atop her dais.

Throughout Margeaux's whole life, Celeste, Magus the 24th had been leader of the Pan-Galactic Imperium. She could remember when the Queen's hair was still part black. The Queen's composure had always inspired awe in her young grand-neice once removed. The more so since Margeaux had seen her at other times, when she was altogether more human and personal. She had somehow kept that part of her safe from the vagaries of her office. Margeaux wondered how Soleil would take to ruling, how much it would change her.

Now the Queen was bowing to her family, which meant the ritual was nearly complete. As she faced the court, Margeaux went down to one knee along with the rest. The orchestra picked up and everyone rose, filing towards the banquet hall.

"Soleil's really growing up, isn't she." Margeaux turned toward her twin brother's voice on her right. "In all these ceremonies, she keeps getting better and better. She's going to be an icon. Practically is already."

Margeaux quirked an eyebrow and looked at him sidelong. "You and your cousin crush. I feel weird even thinking about it."

"I can admire our Scion Princess in her glorious flower."

"Gerard, don't say that. Don't ever say that again." She walked with sharp poise in step with her brother. "I'm going to be eating soon, so please no more about our dear Soleil."

} **5** {

"Was just thinking about you the other day, D." Jacobs leaned over the phronium, examining each through a multi-lens in his hand. "Business has been picking up. All different kinds." He went from capsule to capsule, his head bobbing like a poult pecking rocks. Finally he straightened up and directed a satisfied gaze toward Derringer. "I could put you to work if you've got the time."

For a moment the only sound came from Derringer's index finger tapping the tabletop. He was smirking as he drew in a breath. "Little or big?"

"I've got both. What do you want?"

"I've had action lately... but I'll take something on, so long as it doesn't send me to the shipping docks."

"Easy breezy, D. I've got just the thing for a man of your talents."

From her place at the table of honor, Soleil could see nearly everyone attending, both extended family and intimate court. Many of these found reasons to stop by during dinner to exchange oblique words of opinion. There were warm reunions as well, enough to add genuine pleasure to the evening. As these weren't official court visits, no weighty matters were brought to her plate, so to speak. Those went to the Queen. People came to the Scion Princess to talk about the future, show loyalty, and express hopes.

She ate enough between courtesies so that she wasn't hungry, though they had taken the game hen away from her untouched. She'd watched it go regretfully. But while dinner was over and the plates were still being cleared, she had a moment to breathe.

Soleil looked from face to face, gauging what moods had changed since the beginning of the night. She met eyes with Arkuda, the Dragon Councillor. 'E wore er courtly form, slightly larger than the size of a human, white and sunrise-golden scales gleaming on er torso and head. Soleil nodded to er, showing a trace of a smile. 'E lifted a scale-clad hand in greeting before continuing the conversation with the Orconian natural resources director seated next to er.

She would see her teacher and friend again in a few days to resume their study.

She wouldn't presume about Dragon friendship, but Arkuda had been her steady mentor for over ten years, and probably knew more of her mind than anyone besides her grandmother. As the sole ambassador of er people to the court, and special advisor in a great many matters, that 'e chose to have her as a student was a blessing not lost on her.

Maybe it was all the time recently spent in tiny hill villages, but there was a strange current running through the room. It felt like someone she couldn't see was trying to find her.

The front gate of Jacobs' house buzzed for a few long seconds, and Derringer eased out of the doorway into the morning light. His feet fell onto the pavement and turned him north, toward the residential blocks past the market streets. The business day had already begun, with transport cars and service rigs filling the aerial roadways. There were a few clouds in the sky, but it was going to be another gorgeous day.

Despite his preference, he stuck to the main walkways. Gentlemen who look as sharp as he did are always headed somewhere in a hurry. Jacobs had a tailor fit him into a new suit last night, just the thing to wear under high-profile security in the financial district.

It was part of the deal that his cargo not get aboard any vehicles or vessels on the way. No taxis. The simplest systems contain the fewest errors. It was a fine day for a walk anyhow, and he took his time through the mostly empty neighborhoods.

The facades got fancier as he came into the money part of town. The buildings doubled and tripled in height, and now he shared the walkways with steady streams of office goers. Derringer cut through a multi-level car park. Shunning the elevator, he took two flights of stairs up to the next street.

Iljen Square. He stopped in front of an azure-tinted window to check the time on his borrowed wristwatch. The square was the size of a city block, and the Monument seemed to fill it all, a great calculating dome of information rising from its center. They'd unveiled it four years ago, and it was a huge deal, big breakthrough accomplishment for Aquariid-human engineering. Derringer had only seen it once before. The weather was still friendly, and he was running early. He sat himself on a nearby bench to take it in.

It was like a great fountain, but instead of water, in the air hung a three-dimensional constellation of information.

Within its visual hemispheres spun layers of data. There were projections for every planet of the Pan-Galaxy, with tickertape lines threading everywhere between, showing shipping and trade data, politics, even jokes. This was all changing position according to a logic that Derringer could see but not understand. He just let his mind wander from one tidbit to the next. A little girl, parents in tow, screamed amusement as she passed her hand through a seemingly solid planet. His watch beeped at him. Monument Synchronize? He tapped its corner. No, thank you. But it was time to go.

"The other end of this delivery is at the Massey-Sonnes Hotel at Iljen Square, in a suite accessible only by private elevator. You're the guest of Ms. Karma Ilacqua, tell the front desk she's expecting you. They'll send you up. She's the only one supposed to be there, as much for their good as ours. She's gonna plug it in, read and verify the data, and when she says thank you, you go. That's all that needs to happen." With that, Casper Jacobs had shut the metal case with the data key in it and slipped it into Derringer's breast pocket.

There was a lot that could go wrong. The contingencies were so numerous that they couldn't be planned. No wonder Jacobs had saved this gig for him.

They stopped in front of reflective metal portals. The bellhop, a young guy who looked like a card shark, faced them as he spoke. "You're going to Ambassador's Suite 7. Ms. Ilacqua has not informed us that you require guest access, so once you leave the suite you cannot return without authorization." Derringer flicked his eyes over to the bellhop, who wasn't looking at him, and nodded.

His reflection gleamed back at him, framed in one of the portal doorways. At a little taller than average, he stood sturdy, on a well-used frame. His face was friendly, no-nonsense, with a full mustache and curling brown hair. In this suit, he looked like he'd stepped off his own stellar yacht.

The frame he was gazing into lit up, and the panel slid open with a slight vacuum suck. At the bellhop's gesture, Derringer stepped inside. "Enjoy your time at the Massey-Sonnes Hotel, sir. Let us know if we can be of any assistance." He looked over his shoulder, meeting the bellhop's eyes. The ovoid elevator opening slid shut, and the chamber detached out from the building with a barely noticeable vibration. As it lifted out and up, Derringer turned to the glass walls to watch the square disappear below.

} 8 {

The last few attendees were ushered to their seats in the Auditorium Salon. It was a small, fully-fitted theater with royal accoutrements. A 16-piece orchestra sat at the foot of the velvet-curtained stage. Princess Soleil sat midway to the left in the front row, with her cousin Margeaux on one side and her grandmother the Queen on the other. The musicians continued tuning while people settled in their seats.

Margeaux leaned towards her cousin. "Did you get enough to eat?"

"Only just," Soleil spoke in a stage whisper. "Did you try the teriyaki fish thing?"

"That was pretty good. But I liked the game hen."

A hush descended through the room. The lights dimmed, and the curtains opened to reveal the performer at center stage. She wore primitive but graceful lizard buckskin dress armor, her hair a bushy black mane over copper skin.

The Huntresses' Aria begins with a soloist who plays Lysha, amazon of ancient Iza. She sings of her tribe and the night hunt. When a terrible murder is discovered, the song

26

turns into a bloodthirsty battle cry. Soleil knew the piece, part of the larger Erris of Rahm. It was one of her favorites. She turned her head to smile at her grandmother. Queen Celeste returned it warmly before pinning her eyes on the stage.

Mara Kamini joked that she had performed for half the Pan-Galaxy, and the other half didn't like opera. When she was invited to perform at an Imperial event, she cancelled other scheduled shows, pouring herself into the Huntresses' Aria. She took pains in finding the other singers, for the piece was notorious for falling apart in the transition from solo to chorale. Three months later, she found herself twenty-five feet from the attention of Her Vast Eminence and the royal family. She could not remember how to begin. The Queen and the Princess shared a smile, and the court began to focus on her. Kamini felt a wave of helplessness and desperation rise larger than she could overcome. She met eyes with the Queen, opened her mouth, and let it out.

The private elevator door, the only way into and out of the suite, slid open. A slight figure of a woman in a grey wool suit stood at the desk, her fingers on its surface while her face was turned looking out the window. Immediately Derringer recognized something about her body that made him narrow his eyes. When she turned her face to greet him, he realized where he'd seen her.

Like him, she was much better dressed than before. Her eyes registered a shadow of surprise, and she quirked her lip. She studied him, poised, for a moment longer. "You have something for me," she stated.

"Yes I do. Delivered on foot, as requested." Derringer continued to stare at the small capitol woman with red hair. Three days ago when she'd passed him in the Diplomat's Quarter, she resembled a housewife on her errands. But she was in fact the contact for the other end of this delivery. He waited for her to say something. She could be drawing conclusions, just as he was.

She opened a soft briefcase sitting on the desk chair, withdrawing a computer the size of her hand. "Bring it here, lay it on the desk." Derringer fished the mini safe from inside his breast pocket. He came close enough to leave it on the corner. His nerves were jangling. An alarm was going off, and he couldn't pin it on this lady, or the situation. She looked a little on edge herself.

She aligned the devices and switched them on. A hemisphere of floating words and icons sprang into the air a foot tall above the desk, a tiny replica of the Iljen Monument. Jacobs said the data storage had program locks and tamper checks, and these had to green light at the other end in order to complete the delivery. She manipulated these elements into place, going through programs and items that Derringer couldn't guess, never mind that he'd never seen a computer like that before.

"What do you have there? Is that hooked into the Monument?"

She glanced at him sidelong while she continued arranging data. "It can be. Just like that watch you're wearing. It isn't, right now." She continued arranging and relating programs. "It's its own system. Prototype model, not on the market yet. It has... its points and kinks, but I'd say the development is useful. I keep finding new things I can do with it." She stopped herself. "How was your walk?"

"Good weather and nothing but strangers."

"That's good to hear." She tapped a few things into place and straightened, turning to him and leaning against the chair. "This will be a few minutes." She looked him in the eyes for a breath, sizing him up. "Would you like a drink?" She pointed toward a bottle of golden-brown spirit, two glasses next to it.

The brandy was a good label, he'd had it before on remarkable occasions. Derringer nodded and stood at ease. "Yes, thanks." He watched her pour. Her nails were electroplated, with glowing phronium tips.

He took the glass when she held it out to him at arm's length. She really was petite, disarmingly so, like a fairy woman - but she held an immense and dangerous electricity. He took a sip and licked his lips. This stuff was old-fashioned, but he liked it.

"I'm assuming deliveries aren't your main line of work."

"What makes you assume that?"

"You look like a man who does a great many things," she said, pacing a half-circle around him with her drink in hand. "Usually alone. Though never without help." Derringer didn't bother to reply. She cracked a smile. "Sorry if I'm teasing you. It just... I know the type." She looked bemused, sipping from her glass.

He rose to the bait. "You can call me Derringer." He stuck out his hand. She stepped forward and took it with a ladylike grip.

"Karma," she said with a smile.

} 10 {

The light grows dim through the trees,
the shadows dapple and rise.
Everyone inside, this is a huntress' time.
When the sun sets, and the heat dies,
when the devils awake, but to their tragedy,
no greater devils than we!

Margeaux felt a strange hunger in her muscles and the music. Wriggling inside her skin, she saw herself crawling through growing darkness. The lyrics were sung in Old Indar, which meant Margeaux understood every fourth word, but she could hear it in the musicians, and Kamini's voice. She had the urge to grin ferociously. The Queen was smiling, to her left. Soleil was expressionless.

In my tender childhood, when first my mothers
and sisters took me into the night,
I was blind. All shadow and shade a mystery,
and now it is the other side of me.

Soleil was feeling emotions she couldn't name, surprised at their strength. She felt a similar response from her cousin next to her. Atop that, like graffiti scratched into a mirror, was a feeling that she was overhearing someone talk about her. Like an unfamiliar voice saying something personal, right in her ear. Despite wanting to really hear the music, Soleil kept her focus ready, senses pricked. She didn't anticipate danger, necessarily. If she had described this sensation to Arkuda, her teacher, 'e would have told her this was a precursor to contact with some ethereal beings. As it was, she had no knowledge, and no warning. She was in the dark.

No home so wild and subtle as the shadow forest.
Herald the night-singing small ones,
the dusk orchids and their lover moths.
Let the cool hours envelop us and our
bodies set to the stalk and chase.

With daggers, claws and darts,
All our limbs, the scents and our calls -
only then, when we are risking everything
committing our muscle, our breath, our life -
this thrill is the soul of us!

11

The data on Karma's display turned green all at once, and collapsed into a single flashing dot. Her computer and the safe emitted a small beep. As she reached toward them, a hovercar dropped into view, and the window wall by the bed exploded in shards.

Derringer hit the floor and looked up. Karma, crouching, reached up and grabbed both devices from the desktop. "I thought you weren't followed," she shouted as she took cover. From her jacket she withdrew a custom automatic pistol.

Derringer lunged over to the portal and slapped the frame, calling the elevator. A few bullets struck the frame and the wall nearby. "Did you ask yourself that question?" He got himself behind a corner in time to hear her fire three shots.

Sticking his head out to look, he saw both men down, one conscious. "I saw it as an eventuality," said Karma, reholstering her piece. She sent him a wink before crossing the room and withdrawing a rocket launcher from under the bed. Firing from her shoulder, the rocket plumed a white smoke trail to where it collided with the hovercar outside.

They felt the waves from the explosion as the flyer fell from view. Karma dropped her weapon and headed for the elevator just as the frame illuminated and the door slipped open. Derringer launched himself after her and they were in together.

Through the elevator's glass walls, he could see the wreckage thirty floors below amidst a growing crowd. The sound of sirens was approaching from a distance. Karma glanced over at him with her computer in hand. "Jacobs warned you, right? He should have."

"When he hires me, it goes without saying." A thin red beam stretched itself from her device to the middle of the elevator ceiling as she set another program in motion. "Who's paying the bill for this? Cause it surely isn't me."

"Either my people, who booked the room, or their people, who blew it up. We'll see!" The elevator detached itself from the building, but instead of going down its appointed route to the ground floor, they headed round to the other side of the building. Her computer chimed, the beam disappearing as she slipped it back into her jacket.

"Where is this going?" asked Derringer.

"Service entrance," she replied. He relaxed, loosening his joints and smiling a little. This could be fun. He was empty-handed, only a minor disadvantage. When he needs a weapon, there's always something at hand.

Karma turned to face him. "I can get us out. Stick with me till we're clear, then you're free as a bird." Derringer nodded, though he intended to learn a little more about what he was just dodging bullets for.

The moment the door began to open, they squeezed through and took off down a hallway packed with cleaning carts, linen piles, open supply closet doors and people. Karma was nimble even in her boots, and Derringer enlarged her wake. One man attempted to get in their way, and Karma dodged past while Derringer lightly flipped him down.

Karma tapped a code into her computer. Ahead of them at the end of the hall, the door to the service elevator shaft slid open. "Going down?" Derringer yelled.

"Yes."

"Is there a hook slider in there?"

She flashed him a look. "Yes." Must have thought she was the only one here who'd ever planned an elevator escape. The sounds of confusion were rising behind them.

"I'll take it, then, you hang onto me."

After a pause, she nodded. "Okay. It's on the right." Derringer caught the edge of the opening, with his left hand finding the maintenance rappel device against the wall of the shaft. He hooked it up with the center of the cable, jamming the lever down to keep it steady. With one side, he hung onto the hook slider. Karma stepped into his other arm, hanging onto his shoulders and wrapping around his free leg. He could feel the pistol under her jacket against his side. He jammed the lever up, the door closing as they dropped out of sight.

} 12 {

I seek the fire, the blue-green fire
of Oloa the snake dancer -
healer of our tribe, deliverer of daughters,
savior of lives, shaman of visions.

Spirit speaker Oloa, one of us and not one of us,
with us and always apart, we find her
by her fire when traces of dusk have vanished.
We follow the moon moth to Oloa's fire.

Soleil broke into a sweat. She kept her breathing calm, but why sweating? The music was intense, but this wasn't a usual reaction. Her life had been generally free of present danger; feeling it now, she didn't understand it. Soleil couldn't move or squeeze her hands, holding her grandmother's and cousin's.

Her body was unresponsive to command. Tendrils of panic arose in her thoughts.

Something is wrong, nothing is cooking.
No song in her hut, no glamour of vines,
the beasts her friends all hide their faces
and make no sound.

An arrow! Our snake dancer
is no warrior, her weapons and power
are of another world, why does her
agate-tipped arrow wear blood?

Lysha begins calling the other warriors by name to join her. The music turns darker, urgency rising in tempo and timbre. Easing herself into a state of detachment, Soleil guessed she was having an adrenaline response with night terror paralysis. There was a distinct pulse in what felt like a physical place in her skull.

She would have spoken if she could, maybe to Margeaux, but she couldn't manage even a quiet utterance. One by one, the other women singers were arriving in the piece. Together, they were discovering the scene of the crime. Finally, climbing a peak of terrific arpeggios, they screamed,

MURDER! She is slain. Fallen...

Soleil's senses dimmed as though someone was squeezing her life in their fist. Her detached self understood that this wasn't a mortal sensation – it had a distinctly neural quality, like the traces of iron in water. The animal core of her, however, was a rearing, frightened horse locked in and tied tight.

The dead shaman Oloa was carried out from backstage in the arms of Lysha and Neris. Soleil focused on her through pulses of blackness. It was a bright enough sight that it was something her mind could hold onto, even as it seemed somehow to be failing.

Traditionally, the shaman is a role of honor, the silent star of this piece. She emerges only this once in her full regalia, and she is already dead. This costume, not bound by any enduring or definite character, is often an homage to an ancestor or elder. On this stage, Oloa's skin was black as night, her hair a voluminous dark fall including many strands of pulsating, soft rainbow light. This was bound in uncountable loose sections by loops glowing with the same light, as did the stripes down the sides of her fitted black bodysuit. Their dead shaman was a glowing, alien anachronism, lit up and supine as a martyr in neon; pitiful as a firefly's last dance.

This assembly of glowing swoops and halos anchored Soleil's vision. When she became certain that she could either cry out, or that her mind would cave to whatever was attacking it - the sensations fled, leaving the barest trace on her memory. As though she had eaten spicy food.

The four women onstage were now singing the memorial verse, setting the shaman onto a bier, covering her, and raising her up. Soleil's mind was reflexively healing its trauma, covering its tracks, but she took note before it could erase them completely. Should mention this later, though to whom? Very unusual. The entire ensemble switched to percussion, beginning the battle verse.

We are a storm, the lightning suddenly
cleaving a tree in twain, the sudden fire
springing forth from its body, the fire that
takes the mountainside, the winds that
spread it and the driving rain that ends it.

Soleil rose to her feet with the rest of the front row. She was clapping. With bewildered sarcasm, she noted that her hands and feet were now working just fine. She smiled, and all the cameras looked at her.

} 13 {

She was finally nearing the end of guest reception. Members of the family stood in different areas, having informal words with those leaving. On Soleil's left, her younger sister Mireille was bowing to an Aquari Councillor. Brown-haired and still wearing baby fat at eighteen, she took more after their father, sharing his inclination to follow stories and gossip. Soleil understood politics, and Mireille understood politicians. They weren't the closest of friends − Margeaux knew more of her heart − but they spoke often about matters of state.

Soleil could feel composure slipping, and knew she needed to get out. She put a hand on her sister's shoulder, who leaned an ear to her. "I need to go for now," she spoke quietly. "I'll be back if I can."

Mireille curved her lips in a smile, speaking back with equal warmth. "Be well, Soleil. I can take it from here." Turning in a way that kept the shape of her skirts, Soleil went through the double doors behind them that led to the outer balcony. This open-air walk stretched around the outside curve of the Auditorium building, ending in Imperial offices and apartments. There was a dressing room there where she could take a moment.

The night air was cool. Soleil sighed, tilting her face to the sky. It was on this balcony that her mother had taught her the Alisandrian constellations. Though the Pan-Galactic Imperium spanned dozens of planets acquired over more than twenty generations, the royal seat had been on Alisandre since the beginning of expansion. It was this sky, her mother said, that had shaped the dynasty – no matter how many skies she would see over her lifetime, these stars would tell her she was home.

Her formal shoes clicked along the flagstone expanse. The balcony was mostly empty, but for a scattering of strolling pairs, who bowed as she passed. Rounding the final curve, she slowed her pace when she saw the figure leaning against the rail. Hearing an approach, he stood, and smiled.

The high-dress uniform in colors of black, red, gold and white struck a crisp outline to his caramel brown hair and weathered complexion. He made a bow, his eyes crinkling at hers. "An honor, Scion Princess Soleil."

She acknowledged him, her face opening into a weary smile. "General Draig Claymore." Though the sight of her childhood friend cheered her, she was still dragging, and was sure that it must show. This was the first she'd seen of him since her return, and she was loathe to make the time short; but she had to admit she felt ready to collapse. "I'm glad you could attend." Her head felt light and detached, her voice far away. "Please excuse me -"

He rushed forward when he saw her drop.

Suddenly Soleil looked up, felt the pavers beneath her hands, and realized she was no longer standing. She was supported on Draig's arm, and he was shouting to someone. Soleil began to laugh at herself, but when she opened her mouth it was only the jabber of flames, and everything was lost in the sunfire.

2ND
SEQUENCE

} 14 {

Four of spades. Jack of diamonds. Two men leaned back in identical office chairs, their feet propped up on either end of the institutional metal desk. They took turns tossing cards face up into a hat on the floor between them. The room was small, not much more than a basement supply closet, but it had ambient ceiling light, and the wall com was working fine. The sounds of a traveler string duo piped in, just loud enough to hear.

Three of spades. Six of diamonds. "Think you're gonna miss the official headquarters?" This from the slender, pale blond wearing sunglasses. He wasn't tall, nor short, but he did look like he would bruise if you poked him. The sunglasses were mirrored, his eyes not visible.

"Come on." Ace of diamonds. This man was tall, with a bald head of deep brown skin, solid but not heavy. "Business was terrible. Nobody wanted to hire the guys working out of the old supply closet, no matter how nice they made it in the remodel. No, I won't be looking back." Everything that wasn't furniture or part of the walls was gathered in three boxes, including a pile of com relay displays.

Five of hearts. "Easy for you to say. We're not moving the office into your apartment."

Ten of spades. "I can't afford an apartment."

Nine of hearts. "You just stay in mine and don't pay rent."

Queen of clubs. "I could, but we're saving up for another office, remember. That's my savings account," said the dark man, pointing to his chest.

Ten of clubs. "You mean your ex-wife's."

Seven of spades. "I earned that settlement. I didn't cheat."

Two of clubs. "You sure did. And you never do."

Seven of clubs. "Oh what, did you like that one?"

Two of spades. "I like all of 'em, you're a bastard and I can't stand the sight of you."

Ace of clubs. "Can't stand the sight of myself sometimes, it makes me wonder when I'm gonna get flunked."

"DeWalt, the sad thing is I think you're passing with flying colors."

The radio string music was sliced in half by a screech, and the volume rose as the channels seemed to tune themselves. Both men looked at the wall console.

"I'm on your line, idiots. Did you turn off your ringer?"

They looked at each other. The dark one, DeWalt, made a face. "Sounds like Derringer."

"I didn't turn it off," said wavy blond hair. "Anyway, Derringer. Why are you talking this way. What's going on." He threw the three of hearts into the felt brim hat.

"Listen Dremel," the voice warped, white noise cutting in and out, "I've got a pretty big deal in the room here with me, and we need you to show up." A few strange warbles came through, none of which made sense.

The slender blond leaned back in his chair and put his hands behind his head. "Last day on this line, bud. You're lucky you found us here."

"No, I'm not," the incoming voice whistled, "you have absolutely nowhere else to be. Sending the address." The five working com relays in the box lit up, showing a new message stored.

Dremel sat up, taking his shoes off the desk. "Is that you doing that? Have you learned some new tricks? I didn't think it possible."

"Not me. The people I'm working with -" He was cut off by a twenty second drum solo. With a couple sonic slashes, the system reconnected to a pop channel that made both men wince.

"Okay then." The pale blond Dremel stood, smoothing back his hair with one hand, while adjusting his tie with the other. He bent down and picked up the hat, emptying the cards out onto the floor.

} **15** {

The oncoming sunrise and still-visible moonset balanced each other on opposing edges of the horizon. The grassy slope on one side of the little airlot was just beginning to brighten. Two old friends crossed it towards each other.

Walking part of the way, the wiry, medium-height man crossed his arms, smiling. He angled his chin toward the healthy, muscled blonde throwing her arms open. "Gretz Manoukian, what brings you to Southerpart?" She gave him a tight squeeze and a pat on the back, which he endured with a stoic grin.

"Eyyy, same as you. Unloading government stock." They stood a few feet apart, facing the changing sky. The breeze smelled of evaporating moisture, and color rose softly.

"How long you staying down here on Genoe?"

"Hey, until I feel restless. I'm paid. You?"

"Yup, I saw the credits hit the account, but I'll keep moving on. Treat you to breakfast roast? Heard they're grilling wild runner hens out behind the saloon."

He turned to face her with a stretchy grin. "If that's so, you just made my day." They crossed the airlot together.

Wendel Harper called out as they approached the grillmaster. "Jay, it's you doing these birds? Is that gunpowder again for the seasoning?"

"Yep. It's been all head shots lately, but sometimes you miss the taste of scattershot in the body." He set down his grill poker and caught Wendel in a hug. He and Gretz shared a nod.

"I'll have one and he'll have one. Gunpowder's got all the vitamins and minerals we need." Jay set to finishing two nearly done birds.

Gretz leaned against the wall. "What's the news in Southerpart?"

"Well, you know about the livestock failure. They think it's some rare pollen spread happening planetwide. None of the Aquarii wanted to hang around. Maybe they figured they'd be susceptible." Jay watched the food cook. "Decent business for those of us who can hunt the planet birds and buzzers. Wouldn't call it easy living, though."

"Well anyway," said Wendel, running a hand over her short hair, "these flocks have got a new fancy-tech innoculant. The bio-imm team sounded pretty confident, so let's hope they know what they're doing."

"Yep. Glad you could bring 'em." Jay picked up two sticks and offered one in each hand to both of them. "Least I can do is make you breakfast. Gratis." He hissed a drawn-out S through his teeth. An old man and woman rounded the corner arm in arm, clearly following their noses. Jay smiled and turned the other birds on the grill. Wendel and Gretz raised their food in salute and turned to go.

The two sat on the grassy slope, each biting at the small elongated runnerbird on its skewer. Between them, an open infosheet lay on the grass. This paperweight cloth received Wendel Harper's subscriptions daily, and bundled or crumpled nice and tight in any pocket she happened to stuff it into. She rustled it flat with a hand, and set it to the daily issue that covered the inhabited planets in the Leuko Galaxy.

"Genesee is coping with major geothermal disruptions. Elections this year for the Genoene Council." She read headlines aloud when they struck her interest. Gretz Manoukian stared into the sky and ate his breakfast. "Scion Princess Soleil is back from her Alisandrian tour. The hunt for

Raev Sturlusson continues." The sun had fully risen, shining directly into their eyes. She shook it by its corner and the sheet went blank. "I think that's enough news for now."

} 16 {

Derringer peered down the sight of the assault rifle into the corner of the room. He butted the stock against his chest to feel the hard spring in it. After working a few of the actions and feeling them click smoothly, he lay the rifle down on the large wooden desktop next to the lady's pistol. He looked over at the man holding the shotgun.

It was a short-barreled type, with a carved stock in wood. The man holding it was tall, and wore a stern face behind dark spectacles. His short black hair was decidedly unruly. He checked to make sure the chambers were empty before leaning it over to Derringer's scrutiny.

Derringer turned to inspect, one hand on the desk. The condition of it was unnaturally new for its design; some parts must have been re-machined. "Col, that thing belongs in a museum."

"That'd be a shame, considering it still does what it was made to do, as well as it's ever done it." Col withdrew the shotgun possessively and set it back in its case. He clicked the snap shut and elevated it back to its former place on a high shelf. "One of my daddy's daddies back down the line was a gunsmith. We keep it in working order."

"Yeah, and did your great-great-grandpap sell to all sides?"

"Actually, yeah."

A hallway door opened and shut, footsteps approached. Karma entered the study, going straight to the cabinet to pull out three glasses and a carafe of golden whisky.

Derringer squinted at her. "Did you just change?" She was now wearing a black turtleneck sweater instead of her suit jacket.

"Perceptive of you. Yes, I did." She poured them each a drink. Derringer looked from her, to where she came from, to Col, and just blinked. When she offered a glass, he took it with a nod.

She handed the other to Col. "That attempt to steal this data was so... rent-a-wreck. I'm slightly insulted by whoever thought it would be that easy." Col smirked, taking a sip while Karma gestured with her glass. "Who would be so amateur, yet able to risk so much and walk away with nothing?"

Col polished his sunglasses, inspecting them in the light from the window before putting them back on. "Fortuity?"

"No, Irons wouldn't dream of sending in that sort of skeleton crew. That isn't her style. If it were her, we would've needed the safety net. As it was, your guys never got involved, did they?" Karma tilted her head at Col.

He shook his head. "Didn't have to. What you saw was it. You took out the thugs and the hover. Hotel and emergency cleaned it up. We just watched." A smirk curved at the corners of his face.

Derringer finished the last of the whisky, setting the glass down with a loud clack. "You had guys on this?" He pointed at Col.

"I know, when does Col hire anybody." He shrugged again. "Right timing, good pay for easy service."

"You're welcome," Karma shot in his direction.

"You are also welcome," deadpanned Col. He finished his glass and left it on the desk next to Derringer's.

Karma swirled her last sip and drank it down. "When do you think those two will be here?" This she aimed towards Derringer.

"Chad and Fred? Ten, twenty minutes. They pick up easy, and I'm sure they were impressed with your dj skills. But I warned you, they're only sort of competent."

"That's perfectly alright," she murmured, staring into nothing. She flashed Derringer a self-consciously charming smile and kept her mouth shut. He picked up her gun and handed it to her, holding it by the barrel. She reached toward it, eyebrows raised, and grabbed it. "Are you done looking at that?" It went back in her side holster with a pat.

"One of a kind, isn't it?"

"That's right."

"What do you think of those?" Col asked, pointing at the assault rifle on the desk.

Derringer eyed the rifle from end to end. "The mechanics are smooth, but it feels light. Even flimsy... where are they from?"

"Don't let the weight fool you. The recoil is like a feather in the wind. I have two shipments and no regrets. Made on Geris."

"Geris... the crude ore planet?" Col nodded.

Karma was rearranging the vase of flowers on the windowsill. There was still sunlight in the day, and it lit her hair in a flaming halo. Black knee-high boots elevated her a tiny bit above her tiny stature. Derringer wasn't fooled. "Cobra lilies," she said, "that's what this bouquet is missing. Col, where did you get these." Derringer's eyebrows lifted at the imperative in her tone.

"The Array. I was shopping there the other day." Col's face was inscrutable.

"Well, this florist is okay, but..." Her voice drifted off, one hand on her chin, one on her hip, still facing the vase. Her gaze was aimed out the window. "Cobra lilies."

"I know where to find those," Col said from where he stood.

Karma faced them, a closed smile from ear to ear. From behind her the sound of doors opening and shutting. Derringer nodded to the other two and headed to the entrance. "I know that van."

A small cohort of kids filed in through the door to the viewstudy, a teacher shepherding from their midst. The room was empty of seating; instead, bright cushions and stuffed animals formed an inviting pile in the center of the floor. The curved window wall was set to transparency, with the view of Capital City as backdrop.

Three remote cameras lifted off a high shelf and began hovering around the room like lazy winged mice. Everyone made themselves comfortable, the teacher on a large cushion at the back of the group. When all eight children had settled, she smiled directly at the camera blinking red.

"Good morning, Rocketeers! We're so glad you could join us here at the Pan-Galactic Imperial Court on Alisandre." She radiated eager warmth, her curling golden hair seemingly reflecting it. "Today, Prince Cristobal is going to tell us about the ten federets of the Pan-Galaxy." The body of another camera turned red as it transmitted a close-up of a young boy of about twelve. He looked like his oldest sister, dark-haired and pale, though his eyes were grey like his father's. Quiet and self-possessed, he nodded at the camera. "Sir Prince, thank you for sharing. The floor is yours."

He smiled briefly, rising from where he sat at the edge of the group. He was tall for his age, and the black-with-gold garb that he wore made him look taller. From his pocket he withdrew a data chip, which he inserted into a console by the side of the window wall. The center panel turned a flat white, and he stood in front of it, notecards in hand.

"The Pan-Galactic Imperium is divided into ten parts, or federets." Behind him, a red circle drew itself against the white backdrop. Lines crisscrossed it to divide the pie into ten pieces, which separated to array themselves around the Prince's silhouette. "The Imperial planet of Alisandre is separate from these, to better serve as a neutral governing body. This means each federet is equally important." A red dot appeared above the ten dispersed shapes, encircled by a line of gold.

He was reserved, if not shy; but his voice stayed steady and his diction clear. "Each federet is a common sense group of planets and galaxies. Some were formed when they became part of the Imperium. Others have been regrouped depending on population and transport accessibility." The diagrams rearranged themselves around him, illustrating the changes he spoke of, each shape taking on its own new color.

As the Prince described each federet, the teacher shifted her gaze from him to the city view on either side of the screen. He'd been her pupil for almost six years now, and he always lit up when the topic came to worlds outside the court, especially the distant edges of the Imperium. His usual reservations would melt away. Even now, he became more animated as he sprinkled the cut-and-dry presentation with some favorite gems.

His oldest sister would rule, but as the first boy and third child of the family, his destiny was very much in his hands. For now, he could only repeat the canonical histories as they were taught to him. As his teacher, she could feel his yearning for original knowledge from outside his sheltered world. She had a feeling he would find it, soon enough.

} 18 {

"So you want us to figure out who it was went after you at the handoff." Chad Dremel, wearing both hat and sunglasses, spoke from the loveseat in the front room of Col's safe house. "Why? It's not our uh, expertise. You'd know better than we would."

"That's just it. I thought I knew all the players who would be after this research, but that attack and the way it was done doesn't make sense for any of them. Because you know nothing about this scenario, you might be able to figure out something I couldn't." Karma Ilacqua leaned against the table. "Besides, their attempt failed, and I don't have time to go chasing down every Jack and Jill who tries to trip me in the hallway." Her eyes gleamed. "But I'm curious."

Dremel turned his head to DeWalt sitting next to him. They read each other's faces for a few seconds. DeWalt tilted his black pate and looked over at the business woman. "We'll need an office."

Smirking, she glanced at the detective before looking back at them. "I've got an office you can use."

} 19 {

The place sat amidst other medium buildings its size, an ordinary metal-and-glass affair that reflected the last glow of afternoon. The address was its only sign, though there were traces of past businesses. The first floor windows were blacked out. Derringer tossed a ring of keys from hand to hand. "Well, this looks promising."

Fred DeWalt leaned toward the detective. "Do you think it's a trap?"

"Only insofar as working for a woman like that is a trap. No, this is for you to use. Just like the hover." He turned halfway to look at the gleaming, new-model stock racing flier behind them.

"Stars afire, Derringer," said Chad, adjusting his glasses, "when he drove this up I thought it must be the boss' car. And then she hands us the keys. To a Griffen."

The detective showed a wide grin through his mustache. "Tools to your advantage. You found yourselves a good game here, don't be afraid to play it. Savor this moment. You're aces!"

"What about you, D?" asked Chad as they walked to the door.

"...I'm aces too, yeah." He almost started laughing. "Trust me. But this is your gig." He fit the key into the door, which unlocked smoothly. He looked up at the side of the building. "What do you think this place was? Newspaper?"

"Old insurance company." The other two men looked at Fred, who'd spoken. He shrugged, they shrugged, and they all went in, leaving no sign of themselves but the shining white Sibley Griffen out front.

} 20 {

Residential ramparts ran along both sides of the aqueduct waterway, sunlight still touching their uppermost stories. The water ran slowly between two high fences, contained in its hardstone channel.

A boy sat on a bench at the base of the channel wall. He'd seen people on his way here, but now the area was empty. A beetle droned past, which meant that someone might have fruit trees on the rooftops. He scanned around for public access stairways, but couldn't see any on this side. That didn't rule out the possibility.

He gazed at the upper rooftops, taking in the last of the light. A sunstrip gleamed bronze, transporting the sunlight into subterranean depths. He withdrew half a sandwich from his schoolboy's pack. It was gone in short order and he stretched, shouldering his bag again. He felt almost full.

Looking up and down the channel, he turned away from the sunset toward an alley leading out from the aqueduct. Before he could find a stair to the rooftop, or someone who knew where one was, there came a causeway leading into the bedrock. Down it he went.

The temperature dropped, hardstone giving way to natural hewn stone walls. There were more people in the belowstreets here, where the sunstrips spread their illumination through branching networks around doorways and windows. More and more people were ending their workdays, crossing between levels above and below.

He scanned the crowd as he walked, noticing a couple boys leaning against the wall of an alcove. They were older, both wearing dark jumpsuits covered in pockets. The moment he met the eyes of the one at the corner, they grinned wolfishly.

"Where you going in such a hurry?" said the boy who'd met his eye. Tattoos peeked out from both sides of his collar.

"Nowhere," said the boy, getting out the main walkway. A few Aquarii passed behind him, mantislike legs clicking against the stone, head-tendrils waving.

"So, take a load off." They sized him up, from his bag where he set it on the ground, to his clothes which were none too fresh. They were just playing, and he played back. The three of them narrated stories about passersby until a girl stopped in to visit.

She had an Aquari projection orb. They sat on the ground and passed it around. She was adept with it, intricate and luminous colorscapes rising from the orb in her hands. A few stopped to watch. She held it out to the boy in a scene of turquoise and silver filigree. When his fingers touched it, a series of orange polygons bounced and tumbled through, colliding with each other and exploding in puffs. They broke into laughter.

"Do you all want to come to the Valley?" she said playfully. The two in jumpsuits smiled, and seeing them, the boy nodded as well. She rose, brushing dust off her rag-stitched skirt and placing the orb in a belt pouch. Without another word, they followed her lead.

After following for miles of alleys and innumerable corners, ladders, and staircases, he found himself tagging along, ready to locate his whereabouts should he need to. This might have troubled him, but he decided the only way they might actually get there was if he stopped worrying about it. He was having a good time along the way.

The four of them occasionally emerged onto the surface, popping up in different neighborhoods. He lost count of the new faces he'd met at the houses and porches where they stopped to talk. Their smiles grew wide. Finally, they went through a door that looked like any other door, and he realized they'd arrived.

In a mudroom decorated with lights and branches they took off their shoes, adding them to the small mountain of footwear. Stepping in from there, he felt his soles touch soil and grass. Astonished, he looked up straight into the night sky. This was a courtyard, an orchard brimming with gardens, all lit by lamps and lights hanging from the trees. Heads turned to see them enter, and the four of them raised their hands in greeting.

} 21 {

KI: So is it what you needed to move forward?

AS: This will give us at least four new streams of information in our reconnaissance soundings that should tell us where and how to modulate our power workings. It's priceless, Karma. Good work.

KI: Don't thank me. I was just the go-fer. I'm sure the author would be proud, if he weren't dead.

Karma Ilacqua sat in sunglasses before the Iljen Monument, a stylish cap covering her red bob. The morning rush was dying down. Above her level gaze, they had already replaced the windows on her last room at the Massey-Sonnes Hotel. She read the discussion on the inside of her dark lenses.

AS: If the Foundational fanatics hadn't set the hit on him, he might be here doing this with us. He would have been. If only.

KI: Well your team, whoever they are. I'm betting they've got what it takes.

AS: If we don't, nobody does.

KI: Then it's a good thing no one knows who you are, where you are, or what you're up to. How are you holding up in the middle of secret nowhere?

AS: Getting hardly any sleep, living the dream. Only I ran out of my favorite gin.

KI: Shame on them. Do I need to send you a care package through those company messengers?

AS: You should, and also I want cookies. I gotta go.

Closing her fists, Karma turned off the impulse readings of her glasses' biosys. Reaching up, she took them off and rubbed her eyes. Idly, she scanned the rotating planet of information that was the Monument. The visual representation of Genesee, close by on her right, was pulsing red over half its surface. Shielded areas in color patterns of specific agencies indicated emergency relief. A paltry few of the planet's tradelines still showed activity to the dozens of other entities.

She considered pulling up the infopoints on her handheld
when a muted clash of cymbals issued out of it. A message
from her boss at Plexus. She pursed her lips to one side and
put her sunglasses back on, pulling it into view.

-Saris to Ilacqua
-Please report to the Mainstation in 5th Alisandrian orbit.
You are to coordinate distraction teams aimed at Fortuity and
Seven Suns. Compile dossiers.

Karma threw her head back in seeming exasperation,
but she wore a closed-lipped smile that lingered as she tucked
her shades into a coat pocket. She stood and stretched,
looking around as a flytaxi came to rest directly in front of
her. Nearby pedestrians looked to see who it was. The door
opened, and Ilacqua stepped inside.

3RD SEQUENCE

} 22 {

A searing, endless brilliance stretches in every direction. The pain of it is unavoidable, like pupils bare to the sun.

Once every eternity, it pulses. Magnesium-magma veins seep in for brief moments, giving way once more to inchoate light.

With each pulse, the bonfire rivers crackle and grow. The formations change, a message reaching through the empty channel. An unknown mental signature.

An emotion forms, the feeling of a child toward fire after having felt its burn. The pulsing gains wild velocity, a sense of familiarity growing ever nearer. The heat of a gaze on one's back; ancient thoughts in living whispers, flickering. Getting warmer.

Then like a skull split, a ribcage opening, the scene unfolds and begins to make sense. Faces like her own, and the damning eyes of others all around.

} 23 {

An audio newscast played quietly in the dim room. Mireille reclined in a chair next to the bed where her older sister lay still. Facedown on her lap was an open history textbook on the Phiroen Era of Magus expansion, when a group of imperial fleet officers staged a military revolt. The orb embedded at the top of the curved ceiling pulsed its light in theta rhythms.

A knock on the door. Mireille rose, setting the book down. She opened the door a few inches, then all the way, letting the visitor in. "General Claymore. Draig."

He stepped forward, his eyes on Soleil beneath the covers. He turned his head to nod back. "Princessa Mireille. How's she doing?"

They kept their voices quiet, both watching the bed. "Her vitals are fine, but we still can't wake her."

"I don't know what happened there. She looked tired, but that was all. She collapsed mid-sentence. I think she was conscious for a few moments more before she passed out entirely." His brow furrowed. "This hasn't ever happened before, right?"

Mireille shook her head. "No. No, she's never just fallen like that. These ceremonies hardly phase her, I can't explain it. I just hope she wakes up soon."

After a moment, Draig cleared his throat. "Do you want someone to relieve you here?"

She smiled. "No, thank you. I'm catching up on my history, anyhow." She gestured to the facedown book. "Get some rest. We may need your help later."

} 24 {

Every visual detail is made of living fire. Twenty-four people stand, arrayed as though in ceremonial reception. Waves of heat blur their faces. Most are female, some male. All connected with ties like bones of starlight.

She sees them from every angle, through the vantage of an invisible surrounding mob. Eyes seething with condemnation, demanding testimony.

A face comes into focus. Though she barely recognizes it, it is one of her ancestors. The likeness bears little resemblance to the historical paintings or projections. It looks wrong. As she looks on the rest, so they return her gaze. She feels herself drawing strength from a belonging that always fostered her, while the surrounding forces swell into a roar held barely at bay.

Everything she knows about her family begins to illustrate itself in fiery lines around their forms. Flourishes of their proudest accomplishments multiply into a great mass. She draws herself into it, a comforting blanket to shield her from those other eyes.

} **25** {

A knot of serious-faced people held conversation near the doorway, where an obsidian and hematite mosaic spiraled out from a corner. Those rocks were the ubiquitous rubble by-product of the construction of Anzi and its suburbs. Fragrant herbs grew from the cracks amid the feet of those conversing.

A stone's throw away, he looked up from his task of grinding powder apples to watch them. The sun shone through a quickly moving layer of overcast. He poured a heap of powder, seeds, and skins through a strainer, sifting the

powder into the bowl below. He winnowed the strainer so the
light, dry skins lay on top, brushing those off into a bag for
tea. The seeds went into a jar, which would find its place in
the shed where other full seed jars lay dormant.

He looked up in time to see the messenger lift his hand in
farewell before hurrying out, probably heading to as many
places as he could hit. The four or five who talked with him
dispersed slowly, faces thoughtful. Cheli, in her rag-stitched
skirt, met his eye and smiled, heading over.

"Thanks for doing that, Toller." She took a pinch of
powder apple from the bowl and brought it to her tongue. She
smacked her lips with appreciation. "Good for cereal, sauce,
pudding, baking and it never goes bad." Cheli took another
dip into the bowl.

He followed suit, taking a taste of his work. The graininess
sweetened and melted, with hints of dry spice. He could hear
voices murmuring around the valley. "What was that about?
At the door."

Cheli crossed her arms and sighed, affecting nonchalance.
"The Zendris Fault is moving. The one that runs right by
this city." He blinked. Toller wasn't really surprised that
the planetwide catastrophes had reached him. Places he
once knew had been demolished by earthquake or buried
in eruption, news he'd already been accepting. "No official
announcements, but people are getting ready. Evacuation

within the week, probably. Who knows when these things really happen. Could be tomorrow."

"Could be." He smiled at Cheli. If nature claimed the city before he left this garden, he could think of worse places to be buried.

"Mmm hmm." Cheli bent to pick up the bowl of powder apple. "Want to make some pudding?"

} 26 {

As though the four of them were at lunch around the table, the Princess' mother, sister, and cousin sat around her bed. They discussed recent alliance changes in the Council, trade shifts, and diplomatic appointments. Queen Ascendant Charlotte seemed unwilling to touch on the subject of her daughter's comatose condition; the most she could do was include Soleil in state affairs as she normally did. She sat upright in spotless white and gold robes, looking much as she did at the head of Council.

In contrast, Mireille sat upright in pajamas, her hair undone, though she looked pleased to be talking with her mother. Her last visit had been four days ago already, the night Soleil had fallen ill. The Queen Ascendant had been required on emergency matters in the Expansion 6 Federet. She brought them news, and more than that, the presence of her monumental stiff upper lip.

Margeaux had brought a favorite dress obi of Soleil's; it was draped across the bed so she would see it when she woke. Soleil's long black hair lay neatly plaited down her chest.

"... About fifteen percent of the refugees are choosing to relocate to underpopulated worlds in the Archipelago Federet. There are plenty of agricultural and industrial opportunities there." Charlotte pursed her lips. "While the rest remain in orbit for now."

"What about Zerite production?" Mireille looked to her mother. "Genesee is still our sole source, correct?"

"Correct. Production has halted completely. The Aquari Sendsingers will have to make do with the Zerite that's already in the market. There's plenty there. But the fact of a finite quantity will raise the price of Inter-Fed travel." Charlotte patted and stroked Soleil's limp hand. "Zerite isn't strictly necessary to enable the TransNet, but without it the Sendsingers would be taxed to their limits. It's a good thing we don't need much, and it's one of the longest-lasting on the phronium spectrum." As soon as he finished her sentence, a patterned knock sounded at the door.

"It's time for me to go." The Queen Ascendant rose, and the two younger ladies stood with her. She smoothed a hand over Soleil's forehead before leaning in to give it a kiss. "My strong daughter." She gave warm farewells to the other two girls before making her exit.

Mireille crossed her arms over her chest and looked over at Margeaux, who seemed a bit overwhelmed. Her lips twisted into a wry smile. "Mother's milk, Cousin. Mother's milk."

Margeaux gave her head a shake as if to clear it. She curtseyed to her cousin. "I must be going as well, Mireille. May the light of the Pan-Galactic suns shine on you both."

} 27 {

From within the comfort of the known, her gaze is drawn outward by the insistent presence of the surrounding watchers.

Strange stars shine through the pervasive medium of fire. She knows the charts, and this multitude of skies is wholly unfamiliar. Unknown populations push forth just beyond comprehension.

An individual coalesces in the forefront. Not visible, just the feel of someone human – a mental handshake reminiscent of moondust, engine grit, and distance. Cold but firm. It stretches wide into a smile, indicating much to be told.

The touch leads her to someone nearby. An introduction of sorts. This one is a swell of magma, a wave of heat assuming form. This is the communicator, the conduit. The fire in her mind. It gives her a glimpse of those it represents, possibly draconid. She's never met a dragon in this aspect, the trilling, echoing vibration of its spiraling form.

The trill unfolds, volume expanding to include many strange and emotional voices. They reach, expressing eagerness, a desire to be known. Beneath that, suppressed anger driving the reason for contact, a clamoring for amends to be made. For what?

Back to the grinning soul, placing her again amongst her dynasty. They all look outward. They know why they're here.

} 28 {

As Derringer and Karma caught their breath side by side on the tossed sheets, subdued chuckles escaped from their grins. She sighed, rolling her head to face him. "I'm so glad you could make it out to orbit."

Stretching his arms above his head, Derringer yawned and smacked his lips. "I had to clear a few things off my plate."

"Oh, really."

"My services are highly sought after."

Throwing the covers off their nudity, she got out of bed and crossed the small private bunk to the sink. She filled a mug with water and drank it down, then refilled it and walked it over to Derringer. Just then, the sight and sound of two honklizards appeared on the screen. "Oh it's your boys, Dremel and DeWalt. Let's see what they've got."

She tapped a sequence into the keypad. Derringer began to pull a sheet over himself when she waved him to stop. "We can see them. They can't see us." She brought a hand to her mouth and winked.

"Hey gents. Your timing is good. Your supervisor and I happen to be meeting at this very moment." She kept one hand on the console, pushing the button to talk. The other rested on her hip as she faced the detective, staring into his eyes as she spoke. "Is this routine, or have you turned up something new?"

"Both. Yes and yes." The screen showed Chad Dremel surrounded by his arc of displays and relays hanging from various arms above the desk. He wore his hat, no shades. The changing colors reflected off his cheeks.

"Where's your partner?"

"DeWalt is on the couch nursing a few bruises and a deep, dark hangover. We traced the driver back to his last job at Capitol Cab. Spent some time getting to know the other drivers. Nobody's heard from him since."

"Who owns Capitol Cab?"

"It's an independent company, this city only. Run by the Mayor's son, one Iako Shukla."

"Small-time local hero. He's got no personal interest in this. What about the gunmen?"

"Mercenary types. We haven't chased em down yet."

"So far so good. Keep me posted." Dremel signed off, and she tuned into an Aquari symphonic channel full of vibrating strings and winds.

Derringer rolled on his side to face her. "Wouldn't have thought this was your kind of music."

She lay down on the covers next to him. "I like it to fall asleep to."

He drew a fingertip down her torso. "Oh, are we falling asleep?"

} **29** {

The dragon towered over the doctor, even in the form 'e wore for human interaction. Arkuda had a torso, hands, a head, eyes, and a mouth – all features that made cross-species communication easier. These aspects of er physicality were up to conscious choice, while other details sorted themselves out according to mandates of being. The white-golden scales, the outcurving ridges around er head, and the saurid tail were unavoidable draconid assertions.

Despite being dwarfed, Dr. Basa spoke with calm authority. He had no idea what was wrong with his patient. All his disease tests had come up negative, which was a relief in some ways. It was time to consult other sources and practice proper medical science. The dragon Councillor agreed to do er version of diagnosis.

Arkuda held er hands over the Princess' bed, palms appearing to shimmer and steam. Though er eyes were fully present, looking from the Princess' face to the doctor's, er focus was clearly on some complex, invisible mass of information.

The dragon sighed, breaking posture by waving er hands as though clearing a space on a table. Dr. Basa looked at er inquiringly.

"I'm sorry. It seems as though every contact I could possibly make with her experience is closed to me. I don't think you can appreciate how unusual this is. All the points of connection we have established are blocked, even ones that should hold through any mind state."

The doctor was pensive, hand on his chin. "Who else could possibly give us insight?"

"Bright Wave, perhaps."

"The Aquari artist?"

"Yes. She is very skilled, and their art can do much more than colors and sounds. They have their own means of mental interpretation." Both of them gazed on the Princess in her unreachable slumber. It had been a week, the threshold of a more serious situation. Her even breathing was deceptively peaceful. Though either of them could touch her hand from where they stood, she felt far away, and drifting further.

From the cockpit, Wendel Harper read the real-time data feed on the planetwide Genesee disaster signal. The hold of her ship was empty, hovering light and steady, ready to take on cargo. She held point in formation with three other pilots. No one ship was like another, but they flew together just the same.

A voice crackled in through her headset. "Are we still waiting on Gruun? Ehh. Those suits can talk all morning about who to send where and do what, and nothing gets done."

Wendel smirked at her friend's grumping. "You better be glad he's there instead of you. I can just see it now, you with the IDRA. The bucket brigade to put out the fire on city hall."

A dry chuckle came through the com. "That's exactly what it'd be like. Na. Gruun can do all the fancy talking he wants, he's good enough at it. It's just, I'm on my third systems check since we been waiting here for him," he ended plaintively.

"Anyway, glad you made it, Manoukian. Didn't think I'd see you again so soon."

"Eh well, you know I'm a soft touch for a rescue mission."

"Here he is," chimed in the voice of Emira Rosh from far left wing. The channel bleeped as his com joined in.

"Leiv," said Wendel with a warm smile.

"Hello Darlin. All you all. Awww, but it's been a long morning."

"Sounds like it. What's the word from the hallowed halls of bureaucracy?"

"Well, the Imperials are putting another refugee ship in orbit for temporary residence seeing as how both Anzi and Annan are now on the impending list. They still can't or won't supply any ships for ground rescue, so that's being left up to the Genesee Guard." Sighs from a few voices. "We report to GG Unit 17. They're currently still ferrying survivors from Surcha Province, but they'll be en route in two days. Instrument readings give us a week till Anzi's situation goes critical."

"So we just hang here while the air gets thicker."

"That's right. You all ready to do a sweep of the fault?"

"Hours ready, Gruun. Glad you're back."

His ship came into visual, and they reformed to give him lead. "Just sent you all a flight plan. Let's go."

In v-formation like underwater shellhunters, they slid through the cloud layer coming into bird's-eye view of the stone city of Anzi and the barren, craggy hills around it. Maneuvering low enough to see the ground with the naked eye, but well above city traffic, they followed the line of hills curving to the southwest. The scar on the ground where the fault lay was highly evident; it was already shifting.

Wendel saw the dark cloud to her right before Leiv spoke. "Something's happening to the north." They swung around to face it. Before they'd finished crossing the city, a series of cracking booms like dynamite shook the air.

"This isn't preliminary," Wendel muttered. "This doesn't look preliminary," she said over the mic.

"Ohhh no it isn't," said Gretz. From north to west, a a growing wall of ash-laden black smoke billowed upwards. Booming, grinding noises sounded at alarming decibels. In the distance, through the screen of ash, the sides of three hills began sinking, while lower elevations began to steam and seethe.

Beneath chemical waves of ash, lava began to bubble, pool, and spread. The city sat squarely in the path of things now happening. Wendel mentally calculated the rate of disaster. "An hour – maybe three before the city gets swallowed. Does anyone know what just happened?!"

"Instrument reports are on the air. The entire fault is under immediate and violent subduction. Not expected to cease for weeks." Leiv's voice weighed heavily as he echoed the news. "The magnitude of the tenth anticipated tectonic shift... within hours will destroy the city of Anzi."

"All of it lost," intoned Emira Rosh.

"Let's go. It doesn't matter who else is coming, we have to get there now. We each find a place to land and take on as many passengers as we can. Also," Leiv paused, "this is voluntary."

"Bullshit this is voluntary," said Rosh.

"Not kidding around, Starweavers. We're going into the fire here. We have our reasons for what we do. So," Kev cleared his chest with a cough, "follow me if you're ready."

"He's right," said the fifth wing. "I have my reasons. Fair winds to you all." The last ship zoomed up towards atmospheric exit. This was followed by a stunned silence from the other four arcing southeast towards the city at top speed.

The approach took five minutes. Minimal flight directions and responses were traded as each of the pilots steeled themselves to singlehand their cargo ships through the chaos.

The two outer wings claimed the nearest city quadrants and broke off first. Wendel Harper took to the southern direction. In the sky surrounding them, a multitude of private ships were taking off on their own desperate flight paths. She looked for an open space to hover and take in some people. It can be so difficult, she thought with an edge of absurdity, to find a parking spot.

She glimpsed a park ahead. Torrents of hot ash might be following her by minutes. More than ten, not more than thirty. The growing stench of subterranean minerals smelled like engine fire.

The park she approached had, Wendel noticed, very high walls; it was in fact, not a park. It was a warehouse without a roof, with a green space inside? She pushed aside her questions as she noticed that there were plenty of people within who were clearly aware of the catastrophe's onset.

Mercifully, the airspace above it was clear, and she maneuvered into it.

Setting the controls to keep the ship flying in place, she unrolled the cable ladder to hang just inside the main entrance. She scrambled over to the hatch, and dropped onto the ladder, hanging on one hand, amplifying her voice with the other. "My hold can take on forty people. I count," she said scanning quickly, "twenty-three. Climb aboard ONE at a time. Move, let's go!" She hopped back in, sticking her hand out to wave people up.

Wendel was relieved to see people helping each other on board. She was giving a hand to the eighth person up when she overheard the argument on the ground.

"What are you saying – this is our chance, you're coming with us." Toller tried to grab Cheli's hand, but she drew away just as quickly.

"No, I'm not. You go."

Wendel stuck her head down as she reached for the next passenger. "Wrap it up, I'm stopping again to fill the hold!"

"You heard her!" Toller took a few quick steps toward Cheli, but was stopped when an older, taller man grabbed his shirt.

"It's her place to make her decision. You don't have to understand." Toller was shoved toward the ladder, which he grabbed. "Save your life." He began to climb, numb with disbelief. He couldn't take his eyes off Cheli, who was now smiling slightly. He was almost to the top when she reached in her pocket and threw something at his head. He blocked and caught it on reflex. It was a tassfruit, pulpy and sweet in its leathery skin. Before he could think of something to say or do, Wendel Harper hauled him into her ship.

31

Bright Wave's tentacle lay on Princess Soleil's forehead. Her suedelike skin was a pearly lavender, and the carapace below it was a brilliant blue with a gray sheen. Even for her immediate tribe, who shared a like carapace, her color and vibrational sensitivity were exceptional.

Her deep black eyes were half closed. She emitted a frostlike color radiance around her head. This shimmered out of sight, and a simplistic percussion came into hearing – like fingers tapping a simple drum line. This permutated until all her delicate hair and face tendrils had lifted. The hearts of those next to her beat a little faster in response.

Bright Wave opened her eyes wide once more. With her tentacle she smoothed back Soleil's stray hairs. She turned to face both Councillor Arkuda and Her Vast Eminence Celeste, Magus the 24th.

"I humbly request the aid of three to five of our most insightful patternmakers. I know who to contact." Bright Wave gestured urbanely through the tips of her tentacles. "Together, we would be able to sing you some perceptions. Her mind is well guarded; as you know, we need not intrude to interpret. Alone, I am insufficient. This task requires synergy." Her voice was a conglomerate vibration from the smooth tendrils waving around her head, like a human speaking from a generalized source.

"How soon can you bring in your company?" asked the Queen.

"In haste, we can be convened and prepared by tomorrow afternoon."

"Then let it be so," replied Queen Celeste with a nod. "Present their identities to the head of Royal Security when you have them."

} 32 {

From the twenty-four figures in fiery assembly, one rises above the others. Her deeds and history surround her like a cloud, instantly recognizable as Marialain, Magus the 1st. From the leadership on her home planet, she stepped forward to create a united human empire – the beginning of the Imperium, and the Magus line. It was she who made first contact with the dragons, whose generation brought humanity out of its cradle on Alisandre.

Her visage powerful, hair coiffed just so in her ancient regalia - she looks guilty. The shadows echo behind and about the scene. Guilty.

Soleil knows about scandals and mistakes made by her predecessor. But not all. Far from it. Look closely at the half-truths and lies. The depictions surrounding Marialain purple and blacken, like a fire whose fuel is full of poison. Here is our truth. This is what we know. You must see.

And so she begins to understand the long chains of rationalized decisions. Too numerous to count, masked with the deepest self-deceptions. Heinous actions that are part of the fabric of their rule.

Entire civilizations kept hidden, plundered and silenced, leaders and visionaries neutralized or worse. None of this in the histories. Generation by generation, the blacker side of all they have done covers their bright accomplishments in a mountain of ash.

From Marialain to Louisiane, Magus the 4th, who engineered the second expansion route. Then to her daughter Mariselle, who masterminded the massive colonization. The most celebrated were often the most reviled – though not always.

Arianne, Magus the 7th, to her daughter Arnelle, who annexed four planets of the Archipelago Federet. Her son Ricardio was the first of the few Magus Kings. The technologies he initiated in the Imperial military created new ways of living, but their roots reveal themselves now in a sickening of light. His daughter Rochelle, who established the federets. And on.

The costs of their accomplishments were vast, and made to be forgotten. Those who did not forget are telling it now. Soleil can feel the weight of them, as heavy as the empire she was born to inherit.

She tries to turn away, wishing she had eyes to cover. You may not, says the susurrus of voices. We lived through this, and you must witness.

} 33 {

Outside the hospice room door, two guards were posted in dressed-down black and white smocks. One read a paper stating the business of the five Aquarii awaiting entry. He bowed to the smallish one at the front. Bright Wave bowed back. The bipedal, tendril-crowned Aquari body is eloquent at displays of courtesy. He opened the door, and the guests entered.

They were greeted by Queen Celeste, and the King and Queen Ascendants. By their differing sizes, and patterns on their thoraxes, it appeared none of these Aquarii were of the same tribe. Unusual for such a tribal people.

Soleil's bed was at the center of the room. Her parents and grandmother stood at the foot of the bed, while the five Aquarii arrayed themselves around her. Two more Imperial guards were posted inside the door.

All discussed what had been agreed on. "We are not intruding on her mind in the least, not gaining any sort of access. Merely interpreting surface expressions," said Sharp Talon, the brown-and-gold. His two main tentacles were clasped before him.

"All of us are versed in human-spectrum expression," said Dark Zephyr, the one mostly black with a few green accents, "so we should be able to translate what we feel from her into something you can understand." All five of them carried a barely audible harmonizing undertone.

"But we have no guarantees," said Bright Wave, "about anything. We can do this for, perhaps--" Her octopuslike eyes narrowed, the fine tendrils around her face waving in thought. "--an hour. With some resting time in between."

"You three are most able to understand the meaning of the song. You are all human. We will do our best to act as appropriate media."

"Will it interfere with your work to have a camera recording?" asked the King Ascendant Vario.

"No. But your senses will give you the complete picture as it will never occur again. Your Graces, please pay attention. At best, cameras will provide you with a reminder of the song as it transpired. They are not good with subtlety."

The family nodded to each other before again nodding to their guests. "Yes, we understand. Thank you," said Queen Celeste on the left. She nodded to the guards inside the door, who brought chairs to the foot of the bed. The three sat.

The Aquarii bowed. All their tendrils became busy with motion as they reached out to grasp each other's left and right tentacles with their setae-villi-engendered magnetostatic grip.

Instantly the air above Soleil turned luminous, as though sunlight were shining in from some forested place. A choirlike frequency emanated from the sides of the room. Columns of dark shadow appeared, and moved about as though marching in formation. Out of the choirlike humming, music began to rise.

True Aquari music is almost never like human instruments – instead, frequencies bend, sounding like one thing and then another, produced from the majority of their fine tendrils.

This song began with a sound like wind and travel, transforming into a rough beat. It permutated, volume rising and lowering. It put Celeste in mind of the musicians tuning before the opera, a week ago now.

A metallic melody began to weave itself over the picture, fierce and feral. Queen Ascendant Charlotte almost smiled. It sounded like her daughter when she was angry. Around the melody ran a cathedral echo of awe. The columns of shadow split and reformed, until suddenly they dwindled into the distance and vanished.

Layers of pearly haze drifted within the Aquari circle. This gave way, condensing into bright points of light. What does that spell out? thought Vario, King Ascendant, Soleil's father. What picture do those dots draw? What constellation, in what voidy corner of the Pan-Galaxy? Where is her mind?

Then, a stillness with distinct presence. As though they had been spotted. The music stuttered to a stop and held its breath. The stillness seemed to smile as the corners of the room folded in. The Aquari humming resumed quietly, cautiously. Again the song clipped off as though muted. Something was wrong. The Aquari voices broke forcefully into a great, swooping finale in symphonic meter. Promptly they disentangled, and each sagged or sank to the floor.

Dark Zephyr spoke quickly, distractedly, her speech garbled as through a patchy radio signal. "Not like any Aquari we know. Not human, not dragon, and too alive to be a machine. Something or someone is interfacing with the Princess' mind. Not resident, but more than just in contact."

The brown-shelled Aquari Sharp Talon was on one knee. "Other than that, she is dreaming some orderly dream. We can't say how much of her mind is affected, but she is mostly herself."

"Can we locate or identify the intruder?" asked the Queen.

"In a short while, we can try again." Bright Wave gestured soothingly. "No guarantee of learning anything new."

"We understand. Whatever service you can render the Imperium will be rewarded," replied King Ascendant Vario. "We can offer you quarters where you may rest until you are ready to return at the soonest opportunity."

The five Aquarii rose from their weary positions while giving courtesy. "We accept," they replied in a voice that projected from above their heads. The Queen nodded to a guard, who opened the door and led them out.

The remaining three stood looking at each other silently for many breaths. The King Ascendant bowed his head and said, "I am going to lay down for a spell." He left without requiring assent.

The Queen and Queen Ascendant gazed down at the face of their scion.

} 34 {

The multi-tiered breakfast service was a series of concentric platters hovering over each other in a stack. On three sides of a square table sat Mireille, Cristobal, and Carlo, the younger Magus children, Princes and Princessa. The bottom plate had sardines, radishes, roasted peppers, and bread. Above that was cheese, jam, yogurt and toasted grains. The third plate held sausage and thin-sliced cured meat. The three of them were each pulling different platters toward them and sampling onto their plates, chatting.

"Maybe she was into something she shouldn't have been, maybe she had secrets. We don't even know who it could be." Cristobal pulled down the sausage platter and helped himself to a sizable pile.

"Soleil's too busy overachieving for deep dark secrets. That's how I see it. Speaking of overachieving, how was your presentation the other day?" Mireille stuffed her mouth with a spoonful of yogurt and grains.

"It went alright. I'm not the greatest presenter, but the screen animators made up for it." Cristobal ate piece after piece of sausage.

"You're not great, but you're not bad. You're just young and you need more practice."

"I like doing the research. The presentation part, I can take it or leave it."

"It doesn't take much effort to improve on that. Something for your to-do list."

Cristobal wrinkled his face. "Thanks, sister. I really have plenty to do, but at some point I will... I may as well. Carlo, what do you want?"

The younger brother, still small in his chair, was reaching across the table. "The cheese." Cristobal brought the second plate down to Carlo, who picked up a white palm-sized wheel. "Thank you brother."

Mireille bit into a radish. "Carlo, I heard you lost your temper at a student who was teaching you the other day."

"Yes, but I only hit the table. I'm sorry and I said so." He tore a morsel off the wheel and nibbled it.

"You're given plenty of leniency because you're still a child. What you did was forgivable. But you're on camera now with your brother."

"I know I know I know." He stuck his fork in a radish before looking up at his sister with puppy eyes. "It's fine, I won't do that the next time I get frustrated." Mireille kissed her hand and patted his cheek. He rolled his eyes and smiled.

"It's Pyrean Midsummer soon," said Cristobal, referring to the holiday on which Alisandre and four other far-flung planets shared the same solstice, once every seven years. "Soleil is supposed to lead the ceremonies."

"That's a long way from now, Cristobal." Mireille was preparing to stand in, though she expected her sister to be awake by then. They ate without speaking for a minute.

A knock sounded. "Let's get going," said Cristobal to his younger brother. "Astrography today, with Lector Una Ixa in the projection dome," this partially spoken to Mireille.

"That'll be enjoyable. Carlo, you haven't been yet, have you?"

"To the projection dome? No."

"Well, you're in for a treat. Just don't get motion sickness."

"I won't," he said sounding offended. "I don't."

"We'll see." His brown eyes glared into her grey-eyed smirk. "Go on, your brother's leaving." Carlo stuck his tongue out at her before following Cristobal out the door.

As it closed, Mireille slumped with her hands before her lips.

} 35 {

The planet's atmosphere flashed pale light against a dark night sky. The magnetic aurora was strong as ever, at some points bright as daylight, or brighter. This lit the craggy mountainside. A peculiar fire was burning halfway up the slope.

A large stand of trees was aflame, but this was no uncontrolled wildfire. Rather, the flames buttressed from tree to tree in forms of energetic architecture. The fuel was barely consumed. Loud harmonic frequency distortions filled the air. In the center of these, untouched and protected, were eight beings, each marked in the darkness by a fiery halo interfacing with the greater structure.

One, appearing to be a human man, was ensconced in a temperamental blaze. Ripples of conversation moved through the thick, ornate flame, forming a filigree both friendly and aggressive. It acted like a separate entity, which it was.

The man floating within this sphere of tumult was large, well-muscled, bronze-skinned. His long dark hair crackled with heat and electricity, moving in Aquari-like gestures. Barefoot, in pants and a coat, he floated cross-legged, eyes closed, face tilted softly upwards.

The structure of the entire fire was massive. In the air high above it burned a piercing central beacon, tiny but star-bright. A light like that would be visible from orbit. Even the aurora couldn't outshine it.

4th
SEQUENCE

} 36 {

"So, we're not that smart; but we're not dumb, either. They figured things out enough to get there, but not to get what they were after. I figure we've got even chances. That's good odds, quit moaning." The screens surrounding Chad Dremel were covered in pictures and files. The one he was working on showed a progress bar titled Unencrypt, which stood at just over sixty-five percent. To one side, Fred DeWalt slumped back on a bench, resting the back of his head against a desk.

"This just isn't simple, Dremel. It isn't simple. I'm not cut out for detective work. Devious people hiding everything. I just knew when Derringer called..."

Dremel adjusted his screen shades. "Relax. I'm taking care of the research. If we need to chase anybody down, you can drive the Griffin, you can hold the gun."

"You can hold your own." "I do, but it's not as big as yours." One of the five com relays lit up and began to buzz. "Speaking of your mother." DeWalt covered his face with his hands. Dremel sent the call to his lower right hand screen. "Big D. What's happening."

In the picture, people in all manner of bizarre dress were passing across, behind, and around him. They wore every color of the spectrum, and most sported feathers large and small, including the many Aquarii in the crowd. "--at the Ileus Peak festival on Lurin. I'm A) Lost, and B) Lost. Two different kinds of lost, maybe three. You gotta help me with at least one."

DeWalt sat up at the mention of the notorious planet. "How, in all the galaxies, did you get to Lurin?"

"Same way you got yourselves a free Griffin. You know, I wonder who it is we're really working for."

"That occurred to me," said Dremel. "And I want to look into it."

"Kay. And back to our point."

"You're Lost, how can we help?"

Derringer looked around at the crowds passing through a wide, forested thoroughfare. "So, Lurin has no street signs, and I lost my landmarks. On top of that, I don't speak Lurinese." Dremel and DeWalt were already laughing at him. Derringer showed expression of aggrieved forbearance.

"Well – where are you trying to get to?" asked Dremel, getting things under control.

"That's the other part. I'm looking for someone. They were not where they were supposed to be, and this is how I reached the current situation." The screen picture started to change color. Dremel attempted to modulate, with no luck. The image was being captured with wavelength refraction via ambient moisture, transmitted from a pin on his lapel. There could be someone nearby emitting interference; you never knew who was under the aqua feathers and body paint.

The screen image was now fully tinted in gold and black. "Your signal's bad," said Dremel, chin in hand. "What are we supposed to do?"

Derringer started walking, the landscape behind him changing as he went his way. "Establish a connection with the planet." He was looking around as the screen picture finally roughed out and cut off.

Dremel stared at the blank call screen. "What's that supposed to mean?"

Soleil's mind glazes over. Her emotions are beyond their extremes, deadening under the force of this litany of wrongs. Then, at last, a face she dreaded to see this way.

Her grandmother Celeste might know her better than any other, and Soleil holds her opinion highest. The Scion Princess had learned the world in hand with her grandmother since the dawn of time, and her wisdom helped Soleil build a shining future.

Now the girl sees that this future is built on bones, and worse. That her grandmother knew, even as she was building it, what it meant for her descendant. A castle of blood debt requiring death to enter, crimes upon crimes against her own spirit.

Seeing this, Soleil feels that somehow, she'd known.

} 38 {

"What he meant, Mr. Dremel, is that Lurin has a masked planetwide network or three, and he wants you to connect to one of them. They connect and control all sorts of Can You Even Imagine. Either you're more skilled than I gave you credit for, or he really is that desperate."

"Probably both, Ms. Ilacqua." He typed as he spoke, the displays above him changing views. Karma Ilacqua's face was on none of them — voice calls seemed to be a habit of hers. Considered rude, but she'd let you know it wasn't personal.

"I'm disappointed to hear his contact was awol, though not surprised. Derringer, I figured, could improvise. How he got himself lost is what I want to know." Her smirk was audible. "He said he knew what he was getting into."

"Well, you've heard the stories, haven't you?"

"About what?"

"Lurin."

A sigh came over the channel. "Mr. Dremel, I've heard them. I even have a couple of my own." The two men raised their eyebrows at each other. "I was simply hoping for the best."

"Do you need someone on the ground? Do you want me to go? Because I'll go."

DeWalt lunged over from his seat on the couch. "We'll both go. Dremel and DeWalt, I bet you'll need us both there."

"I don't need either of you there." Upon Ilacqua's reply DeWalt sat, disgruntled. "Just do what Derringer asked of you."

"We started when he asked me an hour ago. I detect the presence of a network like you mentioned. You say it exists, right? Then that's about where we're at."

She chuckled. "That's actually pretty good, champ. Keep going." The line beeped as she disconnected.

Dremel sat back and crossed his arms. He took off his shades and pressed the back of his hand to his eyes. "Keep going, huh."

"Yeah." DeWalt lifted his hands and looked at the office – empty when they'd arrived, now well littered with food boxes, snack wrappers, and bottles. "Keep going."

39

And then, respite; an eminence of quietude overtakes.

Her energy collects itself, piece by piece, certain that she isn't put together the same.

The fire surrounds, remaining. She breathes for an indefinite while. Soon she feels a current of expectation underlying the calm, and reaches out halfway to meet it.

She feels herself transforming. Gently, so as not to alarm. The transformation is a means of understanding.

She opens into the fire. Combustion becomes a means of existence, the world exploding in consumptive and radiant energy signatures connecting corners of the universe. As she grasps the torrential motions that form this structure, she feels herself approached by the people who live here. Their contact to her is like flame rushing up against a glass window. An invisible pane mutes the force into a warm touch, fingertips against fingertips.

The contact is cordially scrutinizing; unimpressed. She is in their house because they brought her here. This is their self communication. She is reminded of the Huntress' Aria, again feels herself hearing it for the first time. She nods, acknowledging the initial contact. An emissary furls forward from the fire, and she looks er in the eyes. A wave of recognition putting her to mind of her dragon teacher, though she'd never seen dragons like this before. The tendrils of fire fold back on themselves, the emissary receding, and she returns to the familiar shape of humanity.

Another change commences, now unspooling into connected strands of idea. This form feels closer to her own. The strands of idea like connected pieces of knowledge about herself, a braid of lightning awareness.

The connection sucks her through into a room of sorts, completely herself and surrounded by people. They turn to her, strongly curious. She is stunned; they're human. She skims her mental file of human peoples of the Imperium, and these are not any of those. Their likenesses flow via portals fueled by constant babble. An unheard language in laughs and whispers, from irrelevance to secret truths. All faces are unclear, and there are more voices than could possibly come from those around her. They are convivial, and critical.

One steps forward and lifts a staff, the top of it a shifting, spinning polyhedron. Looking into it, she is pulled again through those thought channels into the between.

} 40 {

"You're from Aristyd - have you heard of the Pliskin Program?" The lean, pale man in hat and shades turned around to face his partner. He sat cross-legged in the office armchair.

"No." His counterpart spoke from where he lay on the couch, studying an issue of Hover Life in his hands. It featured a Sibley Griffin on the cover.

"It's a charity fund that builds and improves medical facilities on outer worlds, along with other small projects. Ilacqua, our boss, is employed by them as a Sites and Technology Researcher in the Project Development wing."

DeWalt smirked without lifting his eyes from the magazine. "Which means she can go anywhere and get nosy."

"I'm thinking she's got bosses. There are a few above her in the funding scheme, though they're not all in her department. It's just one of Plexus Corp's charity arms. Ravl Pliskin's company."

"Who's he?"

"He set patents on the newer travelgate tech for the major inter-g routes. Made them as safe as they've ever been. Only one major accident since the Plexus modules were installed." Dremel waited for acknowledgment of the achievement, but received none. "That was thirty-six years ago. Now, they're the main equipment and tech supplier for all our transportation networks."

DeWalt paused and looked up, furrowing his brow. "Wait, who did you say we were working for, Plixin?"

"Plexus."

DeWalt cleared his throat. "What, PLEXUS?" He set the magazine aside. "You mean the name on every single drive archway, you see it flashing in and out like an optical illusion when it spins up into transmode?"

"Yeah, Fred. That's who we're working for."

Fred DeWalt put his feet on the ground and leaned over his knees. He issued a chuckle. "Oh, no. No, we're in deep shit now."

Dremel put his hands in the air. "Now you understand?"

DeWalt kept laughing. "I don't understand a damn thing, Dremel, and you know it."

"I know, Fred. Dammit, I know."

} 41 {

It dawns on Soleil that the mass of all she doesn't know eclipses the little she does, even on a personal level.

She feels relief, and proximity to danger. Maintaining this-ness becomes a priority, a good portion of her energy going to that task. The quiet core exists like the eye of a storm as she undergoes further transformations.

People tribal and proud, barbaric and warlike, elegant and organized with unique senses of sophistication.

A chaotic court of creatures made mostly of spirit. Constantly changing shape, essence, and intention, while possessed of a complex integrity.

After these, a human with a particular signature - at once dark and ethereal, naturally powerful. A remarkable grin. Soleil is again reminded of the Huntresses' Aria, the shaman's dirge.

She meets them all part way, the world and themselves appearing to her as it does to them. She returns to the pupil in the eye. A dark, hot space where she sinks into her own breath.

The field of vision opens, revealing an array of objects, symbols. They are monadic, bearing layers of personal connection and universal meaning that unfold at a glance.

She approaches them intuitively, selecting one at a time. Below is a box for them. The chosen objects go in one at a time, synergizing into a loaded construct. When the seventh and final object goes in, a brief superstructural flash sears itself against the surrounding space. She closes the box and collapses it between her hands as she brings them together.

The undersides of her hands glow gold. Bringing her fingertips to her temples, she feels the glow diffuse around her head like the soothing touch of sunlight. Finally, she is able to close her eyes.

} 42 {

The sky was turning pale with the first light of dawn. The General and Princessa were reading by lamplight in a corner. A ghostly light shone over Scion Princess Soleil's face, reflecting off the wall and displays around her head.

A display brightened before making the urgent chime they knew as the change of state alert. Mireille Magus dropped her book to her lap and looked over at General Claymore. In a moment she was by her sister's bed reading the display. To Draig, Soleil looked no different, except for perhaps a change around her eyes.

"She's in regular REM sleep." Mireille searched his face. "She might wake up." General Claymore was on his feet instantly, quietly. Still reading the display, Mireille spoke just above a whisper. "I will contact my family. Please inform the Doctor, Arkuda, Bright Wave, and the medical staff. In that order. Thank you, General." He stepped closer to see Soleil breathing easily before striking a salute and exiting.

People arrived shortly. Aided by the dragon and Aquari, the doctor advised that the Princess would likely be awake within the day. Queen Celeste would wait.

It was two deep breaths before Soleil realized she was conscious in her waking mind, in the world again. The room was quiet. No pain, other than heaviness in her limbs.

Trying to clear her throat, she managed to make a noisy breath. Swallowing was easy. She adjusted to the dim light. It was a deep relief to be looking out through her eyes again. Someone familiar sat to her left. Her grandmother, the Queen.

"Don't speak, Soleil." The Queen placed two fingers on her granddaughter's lips before holding her face between her hands.

A surge of panic woke Soleil more fully. Did the Queen know what had been revealed to her? She welcomed the presence, but her mind recoiled with mistrust. Ugly things she'd learned in her sleep came rushing back. Paranoia took the helm before giving over to cool analysis, as she'd learned to do. Still, she could only bring herself to meet her grandmother's eyes for so long.

The Queen hummed a long, entrancing tune. It brought her comfort, yet when Soleil realized she was being lulled, she fought back. She felt warmth at her temples, and was reminded of the seven symbols she tucked away. They would remind her, and they were safe. She would not forget.

5th
SEQUENCE

} 43 {

"We are in touch. We are linked." The large man serviced the one-person vehicle, readying it for travel. He looked up at what he was speaking to. "I can feel her extreme emotions. I may even understand, and respond. That said, you-" he yanked a strap to tighten, "-have a ways to go in your part of this scenario."

The reply shimmered warmly through the air around him. "Do not worry yourself on our behalf. We are under no constraints to show you our work." The snarl was evident, if not visible. "If forces continue to operate correctly, events will occur with proper timing. Human."

"If you insist on being obscure. So very draconid." Despite being short of speech, he knew they'd be fully vocal about any issues. He hit a button and the small airlift hummed to life, picking itself up off the ground. He hopped onto the platform and gripped the handlebars. "I have people to be in touch with. My supply network, they've bungled something." He yanked the straps securing his packs. "You know how to reach me." The Vedani airsled's field popped up around him, and he sped toward the southeastern horizon. The shimmering heat waves around him dissipated with a hiss. Only the dark plain remained, tossed by the breeze.

The window view from the recomissioned vacation resort-turned-refugee ship Odessia 6 beheld the northern curve of Genesee at morning. Ice caps were visible, marred with faults that could be picked out with sharp vision. Wendel Harper sat on the carpeted hallway floor looking out, her short blond hair coated with dust, face hovering between relief and regret.

Quiet footsteps announced the arrival of the teenage boy she'd rescued aboard her ship. He slowed as he neared her, stopping close by. He faced the planet sunrise, hands in his pockets. He looked as though he'd had sleep.

Toller allowed the quiet to stretch on. There's a word to describe the common feeling to those whose destiny has become separate from their home planet, the new sense of oneself as extraterrestrial. He couldn't state it, but there it was, encapsulated in the moments he watched the sun shine over it from space.

He remembered his mother, the last time he saw her before she died. Beautiful in his memory, surrounded by drab walls in their depressed city neighborhood. Her presence in his thoughts took him by surprise.

"You're sure, then," said Harper, breaking the silence. "You're not going to stay here or go back."

"No." He looked at her sidelong. "I've reached escape velocity. I never actually thought it would happen." He showed the sincerity in his eyes. "Thought I'd live my life planetbound. Took pride in it, even." He looked to see if she knew what he meant. "But that's over. I'm gone, and I think I'll just keep going for a while."

Harper nodded. Calmness surrounded his figure. There was energy in that poise of being, but little direction. "You're still not sure where."

"I never really bothered with astrography before. I could head to the capital, but I think I'd be lost there." He shrugged, looking at his hands before putting them back in his coat pockets. "More lost than I am?"

She smiled a bit. "You're not lost. You look like you know exactly where you are."

He nodded. "It's a habit I picked up." They met each other's eyes and smiled.

"Feel like getting the morning meal?"

"..Yeah. Are they just feeding us here?"

"More or less." She unfolded her legs and stood, shouldering a medium-sized pack. "Come with me."

} 45 {

This wing of the Great Library of Alisandre was quiet, empty but for the two seated in a softly lit alcove. Dragon and human, they sat on the ground at a low table. Their faces were placid, eyes half-closed in the peach colored glow of the table top.

A conscious-subsconscious logic reordering program played between them midair. Its derivatives shifted and progressed according to the pattern Soleil had arranged herself, not long ago in the company of this teacher. Draconid recall techniques had ways of re-orienting parts of a being scattered far and wide across the planes. The human uses supported broader memory, meditation and acuity, methods available to some few since the dragons first offered to share them.

The images continued through their phases, points and shapes flashing in rhythmic connection. Eventually, it ran to an end, the table going dim as the light in the alcove brightened. The dragon looked at the Princess. She sent her unfocused stare out to the library, mouth shut tight. She would look at er, but never for long. It was better since they started the sequence three days ago.

"Would you like me to leave you in peace?" said golden-white Councillor Arkuda. Princess Soleil, hands on her knees, looked at er, then past. Slowly she inclined her head and let it drop, her breathing light and still. It was strange to see her like this. People acted this way in grave peril. She was relaxed, focused on survival in tumult, though 'e couldn't divine why. She was aware and able to maintain composure; still, she had not yet spoken.

The Princess folded her hands into a mudra on her knees, the one for keeping still and letting all else pass. Arkuda hadn't determined whether she'd been doing these intentionally or not. Humans were capable of performing nuanced mudras without being aware of it. Regardless, 'e took the cue and rose from er seat.

"Until tomorrow, Scion Princess. May the stars light your way." Arkuda left, exiting into a side hall of the Library.

Hearing er leave, her pulse slowed. It wasn't Arkuda she had met in her vision, but er essential similarity was unnerving. Was it a warning against er, or a sign that 'e was an ally? She watched to test her guesses, but none were proven nor discounted. She couldn't let down her guard.

} 46 {

The military office was typically austere. The General had been able to give it some personal touches, like the blond hardwood from his home province, and his mother's photography of the Capital city. Besides that, it embodied the position, not the person holding it. On the visitor's side of the large desk sat the Princess' cousin Margeaux Rienne.

"We want to thank you for managing the security and scheduling of my cousin's recovery. No other could have been so expedient. Princessa Mireille also extends an invitation to the noon meal with herself and her brothers. They're dining at the Globe."

"An honor. I accept."

"Glad you could make time for this visit, General."

"You're welcome by my office, Miss Rienne. Give your brother my regards — he did well at the engineering exposition." She nodded and left.

Draig opened the refrigerated drawer of his desk and pulled out a cold juice. He popped the top and chugged it. From other drawers he compiled files and devices into a light case. He checked his reflection in the door of the armoire and exited without delay.

Hopping a couple routed transports, he crossed the Imperial neighborhood toward quarters where Bright Wave and her band were temporarily housed. He tried to forget the things filling his day before and after.

Draig felt giddy at the thought of a session with the renowned Bright Wave. She had extended an invitation on a day they stood by Soleil's bedside, expressing concern and compassion. He felt warm on his way there.

Rasakarya is an expressed portrait made with one's own thoughts and perspectives about their life. The offer of something this personal from a Pan-Galactically known artist made him feel swell. So he cast from his mind the rest of life's moments when he worked like a slave and worried like an old man.

Eventually he reached the curved hall of the Aquari quarters. The quiet here gave him a sinking feeling, which was confirmed by a look from the guard as he approached. "General Claymore, Bright Wave offers her apologies – she and two of her group were called away to an emergency on the Home planets. The other two are currently in the city, if you wish to contact them."

"Alright. That won't be necessary. Thank you for relaying the message." They saluted each other, and Draig headed back to the transports. He allowed himself a pout where no one could see him.

As he stepped into a private transport and set the flight path, he mentally thanked the Aquarii for the insight they'd given while the Princess had been comatose. He knew that somehow they'd put themselves at risk, remembering their harried look after leaving the hospice room.

He hadn't been able to really speak to Soleil since she woke. Whether or not she was well, he couldn't say for himself. He let the roles they played define their distance, for now. If that was the best he could do.

Claymore entered the main military tower at the base of the obelisk's peak. Rounding a corner, he stopped short in front of the Dragon Councillor and Generals Lucay and Iparia.

"General Alisandre." In this building and off the planet of his station, Claymore was called by his greater title. The dragon spoke it with respect, yet as always caused Draig to feel like a boy of three rather than thirty. Though as the youngest General in command, he was regardless accustomed to feeling the junior. "We are meeting with General Ionia and fleet admirals on the Alpha base in the Photuris sector of the Libran Federet. The vortex anomaly there is undergoing disturbing developments."

"This, we need to see." General Lucay twitched his gray mustache. "Ionos sounded out of his hull trying to explain over the com."

General Iparia took Claymore's briefcase from his hand. "I checked your schedule. You've got nothing more pressing, so," he clapped his hand on the young man's back, "I'm glad you made it to our appointment early."

Wendel and Toller stood with laden plates looking around the banquet hall-now-cafeteria. The wide banquet tables had been reassigned to infirmary use, so the furniture here was a mishmash of refugee belongings. The two migrated over to bar stools at a round table facing most of the room.

From there they could see the kitchen, crewed with staff and volunteers. They were filling pans with breakfast for the growing stream of arrivals. Toller took a moment to appreciate his full plate before diving into the chicken and rice.

Wendel was more leisurely about her ink gravy and biscuits. "Tell me about where you're from."

A couple more spoonfuls entered his maw before he stopped speak. "I'm not really from anywhere anymore. What I remember of home is just my mother's house. When she died, I left." He shrugged with a rueful smirk.

"What was your mother's house like?" The hum of conversation grew as more people sat to their meal. Wendel kept her gaze up, while the boy remained focused on his food.

"It was small, with hardstone walls." He chewed, his mouth half full. "She had plants, and posters from around the neighborhood. We had enough. It seemed like there were a million other apartments around us, lotta walking stairs and riding elevators. It was warm in Meriada. I mostly remember playing with blocks, and her reading books with me. Then it ended, and I've been going ever since. Guess I'm going farther than I thought."

She looked him in the eye and smiled. "Many of us do."

"Hey, can I set this down here?" The blond man's voice boomed from where he appeared at Wendel's shoulder. Without waiting for her answer he put down his mug, turning to lean against the edge of the table.

"Leiv. How was your supply run?"

"It went fine. Genesee's running low on its own produce, though. After another week or two these ships will be depending on delivery from Freshwater. Might be some reshuffling of people then." The scent wafted from the steaming cup of joe. He kissed his hand and touched Wendel's shoulder. "I'll be back." They watched him exit the hall from the side door behind them.

The boy next to her polished off his portion with a quickness, and gesturing to the cup said, "I'll get some of that for myself. Any for you?"

"No, thanks. I'll be here." He brought his plate to the kitchen, leaving his kerchief on the chair. Wendel reached over to Leiv's cup and sipped on it.

} 48 {

Soleil laid back on a divan in the media salon. In the center of the room ran a hologram of her brother Cristobal's recent classroom broadcast.

"Primatris: the old ways live on today.
Jennian: labor of living earth.

Libran: the grand structures of community.
Pioneer: the spirit of adventure.
Aquari Home: cradle of the rainsingers."

The motto of each federet was accompanied by scenes
and pictures reflecting its character. A porch swing next to
a green field. The great halls of justice. A rugged mountain
trail. With each scene, things she'd just learned came forth in
every word that was and wasn't spoken.

"Expansion 6: building on a bedrock foundation.
Archipelago: vast connections across distance.
Freshwater: creation, the fruit of the land.
Vertris: beauty, culture and prosperity.
Ferris: the comfort and peace of the country."

Cristobal's projected face was dutiful, innocent and mildly
enthusiastic. Soleil knew the expression well. Earlier she had
studied herself in the mirror to see if she could still make it.
She thought she looked more or less the same; however, her
silence remained unbroken. Not currently an issue for media,
but those who knew her were watching and waiting.

} 49 {

The hall was full now; Wendel had watched most everyone take their seats. She continued sipping on Leiv's cup. She sat back, thinking of old times with these friends.

Back then, she was driving citizen transport on the intergalactic routes. Gretz became a familiar face at the airship lots. He never seemed to run the same cargo twice. His ship was an old model, but from its sound she knew it ran in top condition. He'd sit with her for a cup and talk piloting, talk news.

The first time she saw Leiv, he was one of her passengers. Wearing fine business attire, so she thought him an executive. But she saw him again, on a different route, one in a pack of rough travelers. It wasn't until the hostage crisis at the Iparia spacehub that they'd meet. Wendel's full transport of a hundred was stuck waiting in orbit, and Leiv captained the ship that came to take her passengers planetside. After the shortest of conversations, Wendel gave the transport over to her copilot, and went with Leiv to fly another ship with his team.

Later, he explained to her about the existence of an autonomous network that observed events and trends, and were present to aid in times of trouble. With their combined skills, they saved asses and threw away receipts.

She'd basically already quit her job, anyway.

The mug in her hand was empty. Wasn't the boy just going to get coffee? She picked his kerchief off the chair and laid it on the table. Also didn't Leiv say he was coming right back?

Suddenly there was a hotel security guard standing at Toller's stool. "Are you Wendel Harper, ma'am?"

She turned to face him. "Yes, why do you ask?"

"Your young friend was caught lifting merchandise from a sundries store. He asked us to come find you."

"You mean Toller?" she asked, knitting her eyebrows.

"Yes, him. Come with me, please." Blinking, she rose and followed him through the exit Leiv had taken. The guard led her quickly through crowded hallways to the nearest security passage, opening the door with a palm scanner. She followed him around a sharp corner, where she ran up against the guard, who stood there with his arms crossed. She looked up at a sound above her, and everything went dark.

50

Bright Wave could feel the distress in the air with her tendrils. They suggested that she numb her senses in order to approach the burning Grove. She spent time in a dampening chamber designed to minimize echoic sensitivity. Many warned her how terrible it was going anywhere near, nevertheless she had to. With her particular abilities, perhaps she could effect something. Her Grove was on fire.

She jumped from the hovercraft to the head of the trail, wearing an engineered suit that could withstand the heat. This trail was eons old, and required mature senses to follow – the very senses Aquarii had learned long ago in these places. And so they were self protected by a living echoic labyrinth.

The elders brought in the young. In those groves, Bright Wave had learned the land, and her histories. One Symbias that she remembered had a poetic personality, and was her closest teacher. Meditating with this one, Bright Wave had been able to open new meanings in their language, bringing her to the forefront of Aquari culture and technology. This Grove, in her home river valley, housed her first teachers. Later, she herself had helped cultivate it, furthering the work of over nine thousand years.

Fire technology wasn't native to Aquarii. They were an agile carapid-molluscid people of watery climate, whose voices could connect across stars. Their methods of adaptation didn't include external fuel combustion. They understood it now, but rarely applied it to much extent other than participating in the Pan-Galactic civilization. No one imagined bringing fire to a Symbias Grove, as only Aquarii could enter those guarded places, and ordinary fire would have inflicted little harm.

Now major Groves across Aquari Home planets were burning in entirety. Neither Aquari nor Imperial forces were able to douse them, and no one had been able to overcome the pain enough to understand the cause.

Meanwhile the wails and tumult of a burning Grove drove those nearby out of their homes, or their minds. The audible pain of a burning Symbias was said to be unbearable, the knowledge living inside them releasing in torrential explosions. They were being consumed at an achingly slow rate, drawing out the loss of their living history. Bright Wave had met with survivors to better understand what she was going into.

She felt practically deaf as she approached, following the path by the inner magnetic sense, humming in requisite time signatures. Near the edge of the valley, a wave of heat brought her to one knee. The suit protected her well, but she knew that without it the temperatures would be fearsome. She picked herself up and continued.

Here the trail began to fray. The singer must maintain the connection in order to stay on the trail, and it was constantly slipping out of grasp. Not just slipping, but twisting in ways not its wont. She felt along, touch and go.

After some progress, she started feeling it. Pain like a shock across her tentacles and tendrils. At different places on the trail it came through more and more, as she captured each frayed end, trying to follow the rope of it. She sped along faster, worried she might lose the thread and be locked out altogether. No one had been able to enter a Grove for hours already, while they burned with no knowledge of why, or how to stop it.

Bright Wave ran up against a wall of heat that knocked her flat. She lost her senses for a moment, facedown on the ground, tentacles covering the back of her head. The suit was holding up. Her skin could stand it. She raised her head to look up.

She could see and interpret the patterns in the searing wall of danger projected by the dying Symbias. It was formed with their escaping commingled forces, eons of lives and ancestral story shredding in waves of chaos. The remaining life in them contained the disaster, forbidding entry.

She steeled herself, reaching out to touch the barrier. She let the heat pass through her, knowing it was a projection. It took all her effort to hold herself in place. She chanted a melody, drawing like fragments to her from the disembodied

pieces in howling maelstrom. As an adolescent, kneeling by
her Symbias companion, she had made words for it.

> *Into the ground, all the way to the upper air,*
> *weave your garden in. Your thorns, your spreading leaves.*
> *Bring them forth to touch our living skins.*
> *All the forms that you remember, carried down*
> *and raised in the flowering of our voices.*
> *Here every secret goes and lives it secret life.*
> *We laugh as though it's ours, all ours,*
> *and always return it back. Build the braid,*
> *pour the waters, and sing to remember.*

Pieces of that memory joined with her song. Some were
gone, and she patched them through the wracking pain that
came with their contact. She was sweating, and trembling. She
rose on one knee, then onto both jointed legs, and brought
her other tentacle against the wall. Firework explosions of
color emanated around her as she braced, leaning as though
to push open a door.

The chant amplified in the pool of coherent tranquility
gathering in front of her. Though clear, it was just a tiny voice
under a great storm. Bright Wave could hear herself; it was
enough to carry the tune. The pain coursing through her
lessened. The coalescing pool grew wide enough to give, and
she stumbled through.

} 51 {

As she came to, Wendel calmly opened her eyes. She was sitting on the floor, her hands secured to a fixture behind her. Looking to either side, she saw a darkened bunk. Across the room, someone was chained to a wall pipe. "Toller," she whispered.

Conscious, Toller nodded to her and jutted his chin to the door. Then he jerked his head to one side, indicating something behind him. He wiggled his shoulders and gave her a slow nod.

Wendel smirked and curled her fingers up to examine her bonds. Locking strongfiber loops. He had something that would open these? She watched him shift and work, both of them listening through the quiet.

Bootsteps approached, followed by discussion, then the sound of a key. In came two men wearing grey coveralls off the loading bay. They shut the door behind them and turned on the light.

One walked to Wendel and tilted her face up. Meeting his eyes, she felt a rush of recognition. She had been right about the undercover shipping network. Poke a web at enough points, and the spider comes out to investigate. She only regretted the boy's involvement.

"This is she. Wendel Harper." He sucked his teeth. His rough black countenance showed him to be some years older than his associate, and his posture was military. "We're going to have words about your presence in our doings. Possibly you made an honest mistake or two at the beginning. But now you're meddling. And we won't have it, not from you or your group." Her group.

Wendel's voice stayed light. "Leanders Aynsdotr. It was your patterns that tipped me off. Pirates and thieves."

"Call us what you want, we're not petty."

"You're building an interesting stock of materials. What is it you want here at Genesee disaster? You didn't come all this way for little old me."

"You know much less than you think you do. Don't worry, we'll teach you more about us before the day is over." He turned to the other man. "Well done. Let's get them all on board, and we can go."

She watched Toller in her peripheral vision. Aynsdotr's lackey stooped to reach the restraints. With unexpected grace, the boy slithered from where he sat, trapping the man's feet. Toller grabbed his shirt collar, using his arm as leverage to bring him down. The boy kicked him in the head hard enough to knock him out.

Wendel saw Aynsdotr draw his weapon as Toller grabbed the electric baton from the downed man's belt. The boy flung it across the room into Aynsdotr's face. In the time it took for him to scream and drop his aim, Toller closed the distance, wielding his broken cuffs like a sap. Rooting his feet, he swung it straight across Aynsdotr's temple, dropping him to the ground.

Wendel watched Toller pause for the next couple breaths. He blinked and began to search pockets. He withdrew a rectangle key. "Here, this is it." As he leaned toward her, she caught his gaze with a piercing look. He let her search his eyes, appearing slightly embarrassed. Satisfied, she relaxed, leaning away so he could unlock the cuffs.

She stood, rubbing her wrists. "We have to find Leiv, and the others. We have to get off this ship." Looking at Toller's puzzled face, she realized she was grinning. She raised her eyebrows and started to laugh.

} 52 {

The four Generals looked from the observation window onto a large patch of space that billowed inward and out. It was defined by a minute fringe of light that only instruments could clearly magnify. The four of them stood transfixed. It caused the mind to chatter in every possible direction.

"You see why it's been difficult to study, then." General Ionos of the Libran Federet took a sip of whisky and turned to face the projection dais in the center of the room. The others followed suit, though General Alisandre let his gaze linger on the vortex for another moment. It felt like a familiar puzzle. Just as he turned away, he saw a flash of blue-green aurora.

"We know what you mean now about the ghost ships, the random images." General Lucay gestured with his glass to the projections, live relays of skewed shipboard readings. "In the course of our approach, instruments reported five bogeys, then twenty-five, then two, then a small fleet. Scout ships found nada while all this occurred. The placemap read the bogeys as asteroids, and the network read them as com points." He rubbed his forehead with a bewildered smirk. "Then they started wheeling around like a flock of damn birds."

Ionos nodded. "Yup. Just like that. Though it's never the same twice. The false echoes, we call them shadows. We've been watching for patterns, set some programs to scan, but so far the only trend is an activity increase with no physical correlate." He played back the original recording. "The shadows started early yesterday."

"Around the time of the fires in Aquari Home?" General Iparia swished a sip of whisky.

"Not long before." Ionos swept his finger along the arc of the barely visible formation. "This Alpha's captain thought he saw the arrival of completely unknown ships. He raised alarms, but recon was barely out before displays changed again, showing nothing as before. They confirmed the false readings, and that was our first sighting." He reinstated the live view. "This is why we're convened. We don't have anything like this on record. Not in all twenty-four generations."

"What about the other two vortices we're watching?" asked Lucay.

"They remain stable. Only the Photuris Vortex is evolving, thankfully." Ionos cleared his throat. "Lucky us. At least the effects don't reach as far as Photuris itself."

Alisandre met the eyes of Iparia sidelong before suggesting, "The Loramer Institute may be our best resource for investigation."

Lucay grunted. "What, those softnoggins?"

Iparia briefly closed his eyes. "Those softnoggins have made great strides recently, if you haven't been paying attention. Theoreticians are most useful when dealing with the unknown."

Ionos nodded. "If you can debrief them, Alisandre, and have them send someone, the sooner the better. Someone with steel nerves. I won't deny the shadows have everyone on edge." The younger General nodded.

"Isn't your son an officer on this ship?" Lucay asked Ionos over his whisky.

"He is, in fact. Lietenant Corporal Tyson Sorens. His office is on third deck if you have any questions regarding the crew."

} 53 {

"Down this way. We're headed towards Drift 9," directed the pilot, calling her ship by name. Toller tailed at her inconspicuous yet rapid pace. They ducked into an intravessel transit. No one had tried to stop them. She fixed her mind on Leiv - where might they have brought him? If he knew what was going on and wasn't captive, he should be at their rendezvous.

Toller kept his head down beneath his hood. He eyed people's movements, seeing no one familiar, and nothing particularly strange. He assumed they were going straight to the ship bay, so he nearly missed Wendel exiting at the residential floors.

"I thought we were leaving," Toller said as he caught up to her.

"We are, but I have to get something first."

"Really?" asked the boy with some distress. He recalled the memory of Cheli's face, still looking up at him as tides of fire and ash rushed to engulf Anzi.

"Absolutely. Head back to the Drift if you want, I'll see you there."

"Oh, no." Toller paced her grimly. "Besides, it's not going anywhere without you."

Maybe, thought Wendel. She focused on the room up ahead. He would be there. Him, or what she needed to find him.

From paces away, the door burst open, Leiv emerging full speed carrying a pack. Wendel gasped as they practically ran into each other, and Leiv leaned in to kiss her on the mouth. Without a word, they turned and sped to the ship bay.

"So, how goes the hunt for our elusive rabbit?"

General Alisandre snorted as he keyed his remote data to the small projection table. A display opened of a feral-looking man with long, straight dark hair. His grin mocked them as it rotated around, facing every corner of the room. "General Iparia, Sturlusson is no rabbit."

"No, he is lower. I honor him with the title of rabbit, because when we capture him, I will dine well." Alisandre looked at the senior General's slender face, set in stone. He knew of the death of Iparia's sister on the day Sturlusson collapsed the Freshwater Consulate. The man hadn't been connected to the incident till days later, when they found his signature in the rubble: the trisected triangle with a crosscut on each arm, stamped on a phronium coin.

General Iparia was now the strongest proponent of the intergalactic effort to apprehend the man whose mysterious agenda had wreaked destruction and chaos in nearly every federet.

It had been a long hunt. General Alisandre followed it as the news crossed his desk. Agency squads for intergalactic criminals fell in his jurisdiction as the capital planet General, and Sturlusson was already on the enemy roster when Claymore took the post.

Raev Sturlusson was known for maneuvers that crippled operations, and he didn't shy from taking lives. He announced himself often. They were still tracking the full extent of his network. This one man had made so many enemies, caused so many personal vendettas, that it was only a matter of time.

"We have word of two separate cells, one in the Vertris Federet, concentrated on Lurin--"

"--of course," muttered General Iparia.

"-and one in the Libran Federet, focused on planet Ionos."

"I assume General Ionos knows about this?"

"Yes, but it concerns him little. This group hasn't directly acted on any of his planets, and the forces to pursue it are mine."

"Then he is practically harboring them."

"Hardly. He's put every resource at my disposal and opened every pathway I've requested. He knows it can't be long before they make a point of their presence, but you can't blame him for being currently preoccupied here." They both turned their heads briefly to the blank wall in the direction of the Photuris Vortex.

"Even so. The magnitude of Sturlusson's crimes makes him a top priority."

"That, he is. We're very close now."

Alisandre watched Iparia's jaw work for a moment before he spoke. "I depart for Freshwater shortly. I intend to supply aid for Ionos. Another Alpha base here at the Vortex, and I think a team or two to help take care of the vermin problem on his home planet."

"No doubt he will appreciate those offers. If you wish to send special ops, please have them report to my mission chief, Commander Georg Hertez."

Iparia nodded and went to the door. He paused before it to salute. "I would like every update, General Alisandre."

Returning the salute, he sighed inwardly. "General Iparia. You will have it."

} 55 {

Cross-legged, he perched on a rippling plane of light in a room of vibrating azure walls. His hands were raised, contacting midair frequency terminals. Words and lines of light under tattoos and scars glowed in synch with the programs around him.

He'd been expecting this call, which he tapped to project before him. A woman's face displayed in 3D monochrome, the covert connection offering but a weak signal. He examined her hair in grayscale.

"Where is Leanders?"

She made a face. "Busy. Otherwise occupied. We're switching to plan beta."

"So be it. How's that going?"

"They're doing their job perfectly, which is to say badly."

"Excellent." He drew a long breath. "You know what you're doing from here."

She nodded. "We'll both be out of communique for some time, is that right?"

"Excepting anything through the media." He tilted the camera downward, but the view was blocked by a shipboard control unit. "It'll happen in stages, and you'll be in a position to watch it all and keep up."

"If anyone can do it, it's me." She kissed her fingertips and waved to him. "See you on the other side, boss." Another call alert flashed as her image disappeared.

He took the incoming signal, which was a sending-throughport. From a spark wobbling at chest level entered five gently glowing wire frame avatars. He dispersed his frequency terminals and stood to greet them.

"You're all here, so I take it our trials have been thoroughly successful."

The last wire frame to emerge nodded her head. "We've reached certainty rates on all auric testflesh programs. The mechanical side is functioning at 92%."

"That will do. And you're all willing to do this yourselves?"

"We are. It will work similarly on us, if not entirely the same. Our end of the signal is strong. Only we five need carry the connection."

"Then we're ready." Sturlusson stood and stretched. One figure handed him a green sphere. It gloved his hand in light, which spread to cover his body with a framenet like those around him. "Bring me through."

The six of them joined hands in a horseshoe, and the murmuring hum arose. The two open ends touched the sending-throughport. The body frames, Sturlusson included, together folded rapidly into the spark, which winked out behind them.

He was released by the electric net on the other side, standing before the five who had sent their avatars. He opened his arms and bowed, lifting his eyes to speak with them from there. "That you five accept this responsibility, when it's not even your cause-"

One raised his hand. "Our aims have become intertwined. Signalman."

Raev lowered his bow even further. "And for that the living and the dead for whom I stand are deeply grateful to the Vedani."

They nodded to him, some smiling. "The vector group is ready in the next chamber when you are."

"This has been a work of long years, friends. I walk lighter knowing the blood of my father and home shall have its vindication." The five parted to let him pass, and he strode forward to open the door.

In the adjoining hall stood twenty people in two facing rows. Upon his entrance, they took a knee and planted their fists on the floor, eyes glowing with fervor. They rose and all stood before each other, the five Vedani behind Sturlusson.

"You last remnants of Hirylien. All the years I searched for you, that we searched for each other, precipitated this moment. You know the truth now as I discovered it, and we are bringing it to them. So that finally, the rage burning in our hearts for our lost families and futures can be shown as the grave injustice being perpetrated on all peoples of the Imperium. We are their warriors. This is our first step.

"For all you've suffered, you have agreed to suffer more to bring, if not ultimately justice, then some retribution. To put an end to one of their great poisons. You all have what you need to survive the time of onslaught, and let us draw each other through this fire to the other side victorious." All twenty dropped a knee and knuckle pounded the floor. Sturlusson did the same, bringing down both fists at once. The pounding subsided.

"Remember, this is only the beginning." A smile stretched wide on his face, growing into a full grin. He turned to the five behind him standing respectfully in salute. He gestured toward one, her Vedani hair silver against blue-white skin. She nodded slightly, and all five murmured subtonally, making microgestures.

A door on one side of the hall opened, and in came a cart bearing capped tubes and dosers with three doctors. It stopped at one end of the double line, and the doctors started inoculating them with the brassy serum. Raev Sturlusson and the Vedani joined them at the far end.

Through the door followed a rack carrying necessity packs for twenty-one Hirylienites, and behind that a rolling freezer billowing cool air. The entire vector group had been injected, and a pack was set behind each of them. The chest freezer took the place of the med cart, and from it came racks of flasks to distribute. Each flask was a secure carrycase for a smaller set of tubes, filled with liquids and some powders.

Sturlusson paced between the two lines. "Familiarize yourselves with these. This carries our mission, as well as your individual salvation and assurance. Be able to use them as needed, without thinking, under any duress you may encounter. Put it where you can immediately access it. These will save much more than just yourselves." He zippered his into a pocket. "Assemble things and get in groups."

} 56 {

The three of them stood near the precipice on the facing side of Mt. Kairas, jutting over the valley cradling Alisandre Capital. The sun set ahead of them, glowing hues of emerald green and vermilion. "It's going to be a fine Midsummer," intoned Queen Ascendant Charlotte. An echo of birds reached their ears. Soleil studied her father and mother.

"Yes," the King Ascendant Grant Vario replied. "Soleil, we'll arrange your appearance as needed, though the rest of us will do the talking. We have two weeks to prepare." They looked at her for a long moment.

She acknowledged them in posture, keeping her gaze fixed on the city below. Most of it was visible from this ledge, though it filled the entire mountain plateau. A stream of ships arrived and left from the transport arena in the distance. The tallest buildings of the inner courts reflected the light, giving off Aquari auras in response. Closer to them, the markets, labs, and hospitals. She looked back at the Pan-Galactic Imperium's leaders to be, in casual finery.

Not a word had the Scion Princess uttered since awakening. Pressure and entreaties had been borne on her in various ways, but she remained locked within. They worked

EVA L . ELASIGUE

around it. Her presence was a minimal requirement, while the remaining problem hinted at more amiss.

Queen Ascendant Charlotte drew close to her husband. Their hands met, and they looked into each other's faces. "I'm pleased we were able to meet for supper," said Charlotte, including her daughter in her gaze. She let go of Vario and joined Soleil, laying a hand on her back. "We go now to Aquari Home with the rest of their Councillors, excepting Frayed Edge who will remain at court. Their grove fires have died down to a smolder. Now that they can assess the damage, we'll discuss the extent they can continue supporting the Transnet."

Soleil nodded to her father, who inclined his head. "Arkuda and I will see you when you return." A pause as he turned his lips in a smile. With a slight pressure from the Queen Ascendant's hand, the two women left down the staircase, leaving Vario to take in the sunset.

They boarded their shuttle flier. "Before we go to Aquari Home, where we will encounter grave matters, I want us to visit the observatory." Charlotte clasped her hands and said nothing more except to redirect the flier to the northern end of the Royal Court. Soleil caught a glimpse of the newly dedicated hospital before the medical neighborhood disappeared behind them, replaced by a wealthy neighborhood. As though with the vision of a rock eagle, she could now pick out false facades, poison evident around them. As it also was around her mother. Soleil puzzled at what she could say to untangle Charlotte from it, but there was no evident way, if that would even be her mother's wish. The Princess' heart was heavy in the face of certain threat from her own family – to herself, the capital, and the Imperium, results of cumulative decisions that could no longer be borne.

They arrived at the observatory, which was clear but for guarded entrances. In the great inner chamber, visual was set to a complete three-dimensional of the entire Imperium, slightly distorted to include galactic relation. Forty-nine demarcated galaxies filled the space above and around them, with human home planet Alisandre near enough to touch.

The Queen Ascendant highlighted the Expansion 6 and Aquari Home federets. "Two areas in the Pan-Galaxy experiencing major upheaval." She superimposed the lines, connections, and gate arches of the Imperial Transnet System. "These arches," she highlighted half in orange, "use charged and focus-narrowed zerite for greater stability. A recent archway improvement – people barely notice their travel, which costs less than it used to in time and power."

"Zerite is a fairly new material, which we discovered on Genesee in my great-grandmother's time." She picked out the Expansion 6 galaxies and stretched them to full view. Rotating Genesee to rest at eye level, she expanded the planet's image to globe size, overlaying its current disaster map. Charlotte nodded to Soleil. "Genesee is still our only source, and we've halted production in the face of planetwide eruptions." She tapped the view out again to include the entire Pan-Galactic

Imperium, with Transnet system. "Which means that we may soon have to cut down the use of these major gateways."

She turned to regard her daughter, who watched silently. "Do you still remember the sky from the great balcony?" Soleil looked up at the expanse of stars comprising the Imperium. She stepped forward, raising a hand to rotate the view, looking over her shoulder to Alisandre's placement. She touched a sequence of stars in different sectors and brought Alisandre back to center, shading out the rest of the sky. Three familiar constellations shined in front of them: the Crown, the Wanderer, and the Bear.

They looked on them for a moment before the Queen Ascendant cleared her throat. "Out here, beyond the Bear," she said as she adjusted the view, "is where we're going next. Aquari Home. Their Symbias Groves have been decimated by great fires across their home planets. I don't know exactly how this affects them, but I know that it does so greatly. Their dignitaries have been called home, and the furor is immense. It's all we can do to insist that the Sendsingers enabling the Transnet continue their work." She dimmed the galaxies till only the Transnet connections remained, glowing in the space above them.

} 57 {

Drift 9's passenger door whooshed shut, and Leiv Gruun, Wendel Harper, and the boy Toller collapsed just inside. It was a couple breaths before Wendel picked herself up and headed to the cockpit. There, she opened a channel to the Entropy 8, Emira's ship. "Rosh," she projected, "Rosh, are you there?"

"Harper, I'm here, yeah. What do you need?"

"We're leaving, and you have to come with us. Sorry, I'll explain once we're away. Where's Manoukian?"

"His ship left about an hour ago. I have a passenger, though -"

"Bring em, leave em, either way we really can't wait." As she spoke, Harper turned her ship live, locking seals and decoupling. Gruun joined her, getting things ready. "It's me they're after, but I think we've all been noted." She ran a hand through her short blond hair. "We'll be safer leaving together, now. If we're separated, meet us at this system's freight shipstream. We'd better hop out of this galaxy, at least."

"Ghosting the party, hm?"

"Exactly."

"Alright. I'm fueled up, systems tested and smooth. I'll be right behind you." The two cargo ships detached from their outer bays and drifted casually away from the refugee resort. Wendel was glad for the other vessels in nearby space masking their departure.

It would be twenty minutes before they reached the freight shipstream. Toller stood behind the pilot's chairs, watching the aft display. Odessia 6 had dwindled almost completely, Genesee behind it covered in clouds. He remembered his pack, still onboard the resort.

Toller blinked at the display. Something approached them from behind. He studied it as it grew larger. Once he could glimpse emission flare, he tapped Gruun's shoulder.

Leiv turned to squint at the monitor. A few seconds, then a few seconds more. He activated his mic. "Drift 9 to Entropy 8. Check your aft display and tell me what you see." Harper paused to look over as well.

Rosh took a moment to respond. "I see someone closing with us in our wake."

"That's what I thought," he muttered. "Let's arm-"

"I'm target locked."

The channel crackled loudly as the frequency was hijacked. The voice of the man Toller slapped with his handcuffs snarled over the line. "You thought you could just skip town. No Ms. Harper, you're coming with us. So unless you consider your friend's ship reasonable collateral-"

Just then a hatch opened in the back of Entropy 8, letting out a couple dozen fast, bright objects in a miasma of heat. It dropped suddenly out of path. Audio crackled as the intruding connection cut off.

Harper pumped a fist. "Scatterbugs! That'll keep his lock occupied. Alright, let's shake em." She peeled the Drift 9 up into a cloverleaf arc, pointing her nose to Rosh's flank trajectory. Toller, meanwhile, hung onto two wall handles as the ship swung around.

Leiv turned during the two seconds of level flight. "You. Strap in." The boy lunged for the fold-down seat, clicking the belts shut in time for a plunge toward the Entropy 8.

"Harper!" shouted Rosh over the channel. "Who is this asshole?" The pursuant ship was fast, a streamlined model not designed for cargo. It fired intermittently at the both of them.

"Aynsdotr and crew. They want me alive. They've been redirecting shipments from all over. Their methods tipped me off to the existence of an entire network, and I wasn't wrong."

Grunn finished setting impact shields, and checked his gauges. "Auxiliary turbos are up." He looked back at Toller, then nodded to the pilot. "Let's helix."

"Helix?" shouted Harper.

"Helix!" Rosh concurred. The two ships parted on their own rotational paths, switching relation while expanding and contracting the space between, slowing and speeding on coordinated whim. They were followed by the scatterbugs, weaving a flashing net that effectively distracted targeting.

"I started keeping tabs on them, connecting incidents." As she spoke, Wendel torqued her yoke, leaning from her chair. "I got in the way of a couple shipments, just to see." The following ship fired a few missiles, detonated by intercepting scatterbugs. "I thought this was head guy here, but now I'm not sure." She checked the monitors. "We have to cripple him, ship's too fast. We can't get away like this."

"Breaking out," replied Rosh. She pulled a side split stall maneuver that set her above the incoming fighter. "Passenger can't operate the big gun, so I can't do more than this." She sprayed an arc from her forward turret that shaved the pursuer off his path.

"Oh – we've got a gun." Wendel gave Leiv a hot stare, and he lifted his eyebrows and got out of his chair. He pointed to Toller, then back at the copilot's chair. "You, sit there." Harper nodded agreement while watching her flying.

Toller waited till he could make the leap, then lunged in.
He strapped up, and went ahead and started touching things.

"Just don't actually use any controls unless I ask you to."

"Yup."

With only two scatterbugs left, the Entropy 8 was doing
the hummingbird, firing the occasional salvo on the chasing
fighter. Harper could see Rosh was tiring. "How's the
SkyFather back there, old man?"

"Warming up!" replied Gruun over the com.

"Tell me when." Harper ramped up her speed, arrowing
toward the fighter's belly. She had the pistol sprayer and
Potato Gun up front to use, and she realized she didn't have
enough hands. "Okay – boy – Toller - I need your help, this is
simple." She pointed to a trigger stick to the right of his seat.
"Pistol sprayer. Give that a try."

"I'm not right-handed," he warned her.

She sighed. "Oh well." He moved the control and
squeezed the trigger. It gave bursts of light fire in the
directions he guided it. "Waste as much of that as you want.
Superficial damage, but still don't hit our friend. Can you
handle that?"

Toller gave a serious face and a cool nod, wiping his palms on his pants.

"That display is your targeting," Harper pointed. "No target lock on your gun, but you'll see when he's in range, just a second." With the ball control on her dash, she aimed the Potato Gun before smacking in the command. A pause, then a muffled fthoom as a plasma ball released. The glowing blob drifted slowly at first, becoming denser and gaining in speed until it was hurtling toward the fighter like a fist. As it hit critical density and released its phronium-fueled boom, the fighter just barely outran it. The shockwave, however, threw the ship into a barrel roll as the Drift 9 sped past it. Toller saw some of his shots connect with the hull.

The pursuant ship hung still after coming out of the tailspin. The Entropy 8 banked around it in successively tighter circles, trying to do enough damage to keep him off. Harper realigned herself to face them, watching him float.

In silence, a shell of white light exploded from around the fighter and grew, expanding past the Entropy 8, nearly reaching Drift 9 before vanishing. Wendel and Toller glanced at each other.

"Rosh?" Entropy 8 was afloat, and the smaller ship headed towards it. According to a quick check, Drift 9 was fine.

"Entropy 8?" The fighter ship began to dock alongside Rosh's ship.

"Emira!?" Harper tapped the mic, wall com, controls, but hers were all fine. Only silence on the other end.

The com channel crackled again. "Your friends aren't answering because they can't. If you want to ensure their safety, join us. Please."

Harper steered them in that direction. She waited before hearing the channel disconnect before calling to the back of the ship. "What's the word?" she asked with an edge in her voice.

"SkyFather's charged and ready."

Harper exhaled. "Good. Only issue now-"

"Look!" called Toller. He pointed out the oval of light appearing on the side of Entropy 8.

Wendel lifted her head with a sudden rush. "They're activating the escape pod."

} 58 {

They stood before the song-molded door of Bright Wave's healing chamber. Through windowed crevices came flashes of light and bursts of music. "Though she made it back through the barrier alive, her spectral voice was practically destroyed. She's no longer in critical condition, but she must remain here for some time." Lead Composer Fleeting Shade shuddered his tendrils. "Some worried her injuries were permanent. The destruction of the Groves has already been a strike at our hearts. But there's no need for despair."

"Of course not. We anticipate Bright Wave back at her post when she's once again able."

"Be that as it may." Before he continued, the Princess went to the door and laid her palm on it. "You've seen how these work, then?" She raised her eyebrows at the Lead Composer. "No? Hm." He joined her, laying a tentacle on the door, to a responding shimmer. "Though we can't enter the room without disturbing the mending field, we can communicate through here. The environment within is responsive; when we touch the door, we can hear it, it can hear us." Color pulsed around his tentacle. "Human interface is limited, but if you send from your outer layer, your message will reach her in some way when possible."

Without warning, the seven symbols Soleil had memorized floated to the forefront of her thoughts. She felt warmth at her temples, then fingertips as the thought flowed to the healing chamber. She felt surprised as it happened. Perhaps she should trust the Aquari artist.

The Lead Composer nodded. "If your Graces are ready, let us join the Octave at Glowing Eye Nest." Soleil and her mother returned the nod. "You are prepared for the walk? With a Sendsinger, it won't take long."

Queen Ascendant Charlotte smiled. "We are ready, Lead Composer."

"Fleeting Shade will do, your Grace." From the living wood and rock of the infirmary house, the two next in the Magus line followed the Aquari Sendsinger down a soft, grippy natural rock trail. The surrounding trees fell away, revealing a wide scrub woodland vista under a periwinkle sky. In the center of the area, a rock tabletop stood raised over the trees. The distance to the rock closed quickly, as the Sendsinger promised. Their steps glided to cover the distance, their breaths catching his tune.

The steep path up the mount, suited for an Aquari's ease of climbing, went slowly and surely. Atop the rise, they moved through rings of large, stark trees to the meeting place within.

Eight Aquarii rose to greet them from around the oval rock table. The large stone in its middle caught tones of light, throwing them into the air above. They made courtesies, then launched into discussion.

At the Queen Ascendant's behest, they outlined the extent of the disasters. The fires had touched the Groves of every home planet. "They are not just places. The Symbias Trees are part of how we gain our adult capabilities, our full range of communication. We have a connection with these that only grows stronger as we age. The Symbias keep and pass on much of our memory. Those of us connected to Groves that burned are variously debilitated. Scant few of us are unaffected."

They turned down the Queen's offer of medical support. These kinds of injury, they explained, were only treatable by Aquari methods. Instead, they requested botanical researchers and investigators. "We want to know how this happened, and how to rebuild. We haven't seen this kind of destruction to the Symbias since we became a people."

The nine Aquarii exchanged the lead expressing their viewpoints to the Queen Ascendant. "Most may find it difficult to continue our occupations. I advise summoning a replacement force where possible. Many of us will have to return home, no question."

"And what about professions with no non-Aquari equivalents?" He knew she meant specifically the Sendsingers. These Aquarii, in concert with human technologies, enabled transit and trade throughout the Pan-Galaxy with their spacefaring voices. These specialists swore allegiance to no one planet. The Sendsinger's Guild was represented as a planet unto itself at the Aquari Home Federet - the ninth member of an Octave.

Lead Composer Fleeting Shade rose from his seat. "I attest to the difficulty of singing across the stars without connection to the Symbias of one's youth." His crowning tendrils wavered with uncompressed grief, his two tentacles clasped before him. His emitted spectrum was deeply clouded with grey. "Not that we can't do it. We'll tire easily. With the support we can find amongst ourselves, there may be a quarter loss in service power until we recover more fully."

Queen Ascendant Charlotte blinked, taken aback. "A quarter."

Fleeting Shade bowed deeply. "Only one quarter, with the Guild doing all it can to mitigate widespread injury." They went on to discuss adjusting travel regulations. The bright stone in the table threw strands and loops of light in the space around them. The others touched this stone without a thought, and Soleil reached out to do the same. It was warm, and like water, there were currents below the surface.

"If we are ready to conclude," said the Lead Composer, "touch the shore stone, focus, and the session will construct itself." Nine Aquarii and two humans placed their digits on the edge of the lit stone, and a full image blossomed above them. Their eleven perspectives shifted through various balances, moving thought elements to achieve relation. As greater patterns emerged, the stone emitted bright, warm pulses.

The Scion Princess opened up to the Rasakarya, thinking something might float out to jar her speech. No such surprise, but her impression of the conversation became more detailed and true to memory, with added nuances from the thoughts of others. After the final harmonic burst, she disconnected.

From within the escape pod, the two women watched the nearby dogfight between Harper's Drift 9 and their attacker. There wasn't much debris nearby, so Harper used the Entropy 8 as a maneuvering focus. Rosh watched shots fire past the hull of her ship with clenching fists. "Where's that gun of yours. Quit dancing."

The attacking fighter popped in from a blind angle, straight toward the window of the pod. There was a split second to grab hold before the blow sent them careening.

"I think it fair, perhaps, to discount your trip fee," Rosh breathed as the pod slowed itself.

"It's my rotten luck." The passenger, a lovely woman though currently disheveled, shot her a fey look. "Listen, if we get through this, I will pay double." She sighed and muttered.

The window drifted round in time to see the fighter release a beam that stretched into a razor-thin plane. Drift 9 dove out of the way, but Rosh's ship was helpless in its path. "No stop – why -" She watched the beam fatally interrupt both of her engines. "ENTROPY," Rosh wailed as her machinery crumbled.

A wide white flash suddenly cut across their field of vision. The fighter wobbled past, now missing part of a scorpion wing. Another gigantic beam flashed out of the Drift 9, making a square hit before anyone could blink. The fighter just drifted now, leaking fuel into space, the rear of it shredded.

The two looked at each other, holding their breaths. Drift 9 popped up in front of them, hatch open to swallow them.

After steadying the pod inside, Leiv Gruun opened the door. The passenger exited, staggering over to sit on a nearby cargo case. As Rosh stepped out, she clapped Gruun on the shoulder. "SkyFather?"

Leiv nodded and grinned. He was a crack shot with that beast of a thing, she knew from the time they went asteroid shooting. Emira felt the ship beneath her on its way into the next neighborhood.

The green-haired passenger looked up from where she sat. "Where are we headed right now?"

"Out of here, first," Emira Rosh replied. "After that," she looked at Gruun, "we'll talk it over."

"I'd like to discuss it before we go very much further." She stood and approached them. "My errand is urgent."

Leiv and Emira gave each other a look. "We'll take it to the captain," he said, gesturing for them to follow.

Toller vacated the copilot's chair when the three of them entered. Leiv touched Wendel on the shoulder before he took the seat. She unbuckled and embraced Emira. "I'm sorry about your ship."

Emira began the laughter, but they both carried it for a moment. "Ah. I've caught up with you. Now we'll both have nines."

"Great number. Badge of pride." Wendel wiped her eye.

Emira indicated her passenger. "This is Arcta Hydraia. She's looking to contract a private transport."

"Nice to meet you, Ms. Hydraia. You've found the best ship round these parts." The two of them enjoyed the joke. "Well, where is it you're headed?"

She drew herself up, smoothing her hair. "To Alisandre Capital, with haste."

6th SEQUENCE

} 60 {

The light streamed through the holes in the cave ceiling as it bounced off the pool of water and onto the walls. Past where her toes dabbled, Karma Ilacqua watched gold and white fish nibble larva from the surface.

"We've been lucky twice already." She sipped her fizzy beverage and looked sidelong at the mustached detective. "With finding the system taproot, and unearthing the Hoopoe in that tent. Blasted kid, sending us on a goose chase."

Derringer aimed a level gaze at her from where he sat in his shorts under a ray of sunlight. "What do you expect, he's from here."

"Yeah, I'm sorry you didn't learn that sooner. We got a little worried, but he's going to hold up his end after all."

"You think so?"

"Oh yeah, he wouldn't have boarded the jet at all otherwise."

"You know - I helped this happen, but I still don't really know what it was all about."

"You wouldn't want to. The clearance levels aren't worth your trouble."

Derringer leaned back against the knobbly-smooth cave wall and sipped his liquor. "I guessed that."

"You're not bad at doing the dirty work, Derringer."

"My specialty, madame." He raised his glass in a toast.

Karma cupped water in a hand and poured it over her legs. The computer projected a message to her right. "Our intrepid backup." She keyed a sequence to show the incoming images without displaying their own. "Greetings, gentlemen. Do you find the compensation satisfactory?"

"Shit yes, Ms. Ilacqua. Shit yes." Fred DeWalt's reply piped in with satisfaction.

"Enjoy your new office. My associates and I may be in touch further down the line."

Chad Dremel nudged his partner out of the screen space. "We'll look forward to hearing from you. How's Derringer down there on Lurin?"

Karma raised her eyebrow at the hint of envy, smirking at the detective. "He's in tip-top shape, we've got it wrapped out here. I'll let him know you were concerned."

A suspicious pause from the security team. "Are you two just living the lush Lurin dream, or what?"

Derringer leaned over to speak. "We're hiding in a dank little hole in the ground, Dremel. I'll be sure and bring you pictures if we make it out of this trench alive." He reached over and tapped the call closed.

Karma leaned towards him. "I'll do my best to make sure that happens."

"You can do your worst."

} 61 {

Though their passenger insisted she didn't require special consideration, they picked the finest pub in Dalmeera – plenty of chairs, intact windows, no fleas, full meal service. Toller looked across the table at her, indifferently curious.

Arcta Hydraia's long green hair was braided, and she gazed through spectacles at the menu, a mess of chalk writing on the opposing wall. She murmured and nodded, then blinked and looked elsewhere as she noticed the boy's attention on her.

"So you're a scientist?" he asked again.

"Yes, in massive sphere dynamics."

"I don't know what that is."

"A relatively new discipline. We've only really been able to explore sphere dynamics since the appearance of non-solid anomalies." She paused. "And from there it gets complicated."

"Why are you going to the capital?"

She drew her breath in slowly. "Sorry, classified. It's important enough that I don't want to look for a different ship. Not here in Dalmeera, anyway."

A blond figure detached from the crowd to stand square in front of their booth. "What do you guys want? I'm going to fetch it from the bar." Wendel's short hair was in disarray, a lingering smile on her face.

"Did Leiv go?" Toller asked, using his first name as requested.

"Yeah, we found a buddy headed out to join the second round of the refugee shuffle. They left, he's going to look to his ship. Did you want anything to eat or drink?"

"How about a fried honklizard steak?"

Wendel raised her eyebrows. "Hungry boy. I'll finish it if you don't. What about you, Ms. Hydraia?"

"Arcta, please," she replied, her eyes glancing at distant corners. "I'm not hungry right now, thanks."

Wendel peered at her. "How about some hot silver?"

"Hot silver?"

"You can't leave Dalmeera without trying hot silver, no ma'am." She patted the table. "Back in a minute. Don't leave, don't get in trouble." She turned to weave through the thick crowd toward the counters. Toller shrugged across the table.

The pilot was back shortly with food. She unburdened herself of the steak and kept a mug for herself, handing the other to Arcta, who looked curiously at the iridescence in her cup. Harper took a hearty sip. "Moonlighty caffeinated nourishment. They don't make it properly outside Dalmeera, they really don't." Harper watched the passenger's tentative reaction.

"How long are we to wait here, do you think?" Arcta asked her pilot without impatience. "I trust your reasoning is good, I am just curious."

"There are lots of people I haven't seen here, which is good," said Wendel, continuing to sip. "It means parts of the world are in working order. I just sense a simmer in the direction of the capital, and I'm waiting for it to die down. It's so central a place, and also a busy time. I'm not too apprehensive to go there, that's our next wise step fare aside. I'm aiming for a completely uneventful trip." Harper was draining her cup quickly, almost as fast as Toller was demolishing his steak. Arcta noticed their pace and followed suit.

"It's fair to tell you now that we're hiding in plain sight. We're likely surrounded by people who would aid in our capture if they knew who they were looking at. But they don't, which helps me find the safe route." Harper put out a hand. "I wasn't placing you at any great risk. This town is dangerous, but also safe."

The three finished their food and drink without much extra talk. Murmurs rose and fell, deals, meetings, uproar and upset – the place as usual.

At the sound of a shot, chaos erupted. Wendel pulled the other two under the table, and dragging them by their shirts like ducklings, crawled along the wall below people's legs, shielding the three of them with well aimed swats. The other two kept quiet and stayed close. They squeezed out of a door into a less crowded chamber.

Harper yelled briefly to the others. "This," she pointed, "has nothing to do with us. Not our problem. We're going now." Her words were clearly enunciated, her face entirely too innocent. Toller and Arcta looked at each other, and both nodded tersely, agreeing that they would just like to get out.

Outside the bar, the noise was surprisingly minimal. It was a localized event. Harper put a hand on their backs and walked them away briskly. "Nothing to worry about," were her only words until they boarded the Drift 9 at the airlot.

} 62 {

The floating stage platform shimmered behind a curving geometric field. Where they began in the transport arena, Princessa Mireille Magus took the speaker's dais in the center, between her older sister and younger brother below.

The procession aisle was lined with people. The main group of platforms started forward. Performers from both sides of the path joined them to enact the Lay of Sakhana & Zoe, the capital's traditional Pyrean play, narrated by the Princessa.

Now we retell the tale,
as we do every Pyrean Midsummer.
The story of old Babylon Magus,
when this place was Babylon,
before it was Alisandre,
in the times of the Magus Emperors.

When walls, the ground, lights, the world,
breathed and grew at human whim,
miraculous machinery lost to ancient thought.
Before even the pergola on the plateau was raised,
when water reached to the walls of the city,
there was an only son, only child of the Magus.
His name was Marius Nikolai, also called Sakhana,
for he embodied the gentle warrior's way,
young but already wise, formidable in reason.

The actor playing Marius Nikolai leaped to the main
stage preceding the royal family. He bore a shock of blond
hair, wearing black and grey leather armor blazoned with old
crests. Aquari scene artists following to either side displayed a
vast city fortress with lights, smoke and high stone walls.

Clever enough was he to discover the great evil
in old Babylon, in the walls themselves,
forces that held his dear land in secret thrall.
Cousins. Advisors. The Builders. His Father.
Old Babylon Magus was dying a slow death
at the hands of its keepers, bargains they'd made
with forces beyond their ken.

He would witness the end of it.
Clever Sakhana, he made sure of it.
He took action, performing rites for those
he hoped he would save, and wept
for the fall of this place, as he knew it must.

The actor's stage morphed into a network of evolving paths along which he ran, defeating enemies who fell back in acrobatic tumbles to melt into the crowd.

By his engines, by his doing,
Babylon fell in one night.
His Father. Advisors. Cousins. The walls.
Many wonders and arts, now gone.
Sakhana cast himself from a keyhole parapet
to the waves far below,
his last desperate measure.

Old Babylon Magus had different creatures then,
and these saved the young man, bearing him far.
Sakhana only heard their ocean music.

He was carried on a billowing construct of dark blue and white silk, as operatic singers mimicked portisfish calls. When he returned to it, the stage platform was set as a seaside cove.

He awoke on a shore at the base of a cliff,
as a woman was climbing down.
He hailed her, and though hesitant,

she went to help the stranger.
This was Zoe, fleeing from capture.

Sakhana was sorely weak. Zoe gave him water,
and brought him up the long approach
to the entrance of a cave.
Within were rooms hewn from the rough stone cliff.
In one of these they hid,
and as he regained his health,
she told Marius Nikolai her tale.

Zoe lived her whole life by this cliff,
but was now pursued for reasons unknown.
She could defend herself with her bow in hand, and that was all.
Her pursuers were relentless -
they threatened her family to find her.
She was leaving to hide when she found Sakhana at the shore.

Trusting Zoe in turn,
Sakhana told her his tale of flight.
He recovered, and they ventured further into the cave.
They continued until they reached an iron gate;
beyond it lay sky.

Aquari projection made the sky around the stage seem brighter, sparkling and clear. Rays shone down on the evolving stage floor shaping a path. They were now in the midst of the University Quarter, surrounded by buildings of the old institutions.

Light fell over expanses of mosaic-tiled streets.
Sakhana saw before him a kingdom
more beautiful than Babylon.
Gardens, fountains, a palace in the distance,
bathed in sunny silence.
Zoe found the gate key nearby where it was hid,
and they walked to the palace,
eating fruit from the trees.

Inside were further splendors, all deserted.
A series of statues led them to a chamber below,
where a powerful light pulsed and glowed.

The light poured forth from an enormous jewel,
size of an eagle, crystalline and blue.
It rested on a pedestal in the center
of the great underground chamber.
Without a thought, they drew close to this
starry warmth, but as they touched it
the earth and the foundations began to shake.
Sakhana went to flee, but Zoe cried out
that they mustn't abandon the jewel.
She toppled it from the pedestal,
but it was too heavy for her to lift.
So Sakhana carried it with her, though
they could hear the castle crumbling above them.
Through grave danger they emerged
to the mosaic-tiled streets.

The castle collapsed behind them in a cloud of dust.
From this cloud issued a furious roar;
a flaming beast with hooves, wings and talons
came charging with a voice like a host of warriors.

The costume of the beast was manipulated by athletic dancers, who moved to make the stride of its limbs. It trailed flames and smoke. As they passed through the hospitals, troops of singers from the Imperial Army joined to march alongside.

Sakhana made himself a match for the beast.
As bright as the beast burned,
it was no brighter than the flame in his heart.
As high as it flew, it never escaped his eye.
When it closed the distance, Marius Nikolai
leaped to meet it with bare hands of iron.

The male lead showed his prowess in hand to hand martial display. Princess Soleil watched his leaps and twists, lifting her eyes to scan the crowds. They rested again on the female lead in her travel dress.

Zoe stood guard with her bow over the jewel
as Marius Nikolai and the beast wrestled
once, twice, thrice, and each time
his burns were healed with the light of the jewel.
The next time the beast broke free,
it wheeled to face the girl, and dove.
She struck the beast with her arrows,

but they burned, and she threw herself out of its path.
With its talons, the beast seized the jewel.
As it flew away, Zoe loosed more arrows
until one struck the jewel,
breaking a piece of it free.

Sakhana found it where it fell, and offered it
back to Zoe. They knew the beast would return soon,
so they fled back across the deserted city
to the tunnel cave.

Exiting the cave, they encountered a ship
anchored off the coast, and rowboats on the beach.
Zoe retreated, but Marius Nikolai stopped her.
He knew them – pirate traders who visited Babylon Magus.
Zoe stayed hid, and Sakhana moved closer to investigate.

The ship and boats were festooned hover vehicles, eliciting cheers from the crowd when they joined the scene. The salty crew were popular in this rough neighborhood.

He overheard them speak of his home:
a city in ruins, but a people awakened and free.
They struggled to survive the harsh time,
but still they sang of that day as a good one.
They celebrated the fall as a victory,
and so Marius Nikolai knew that he could return home.

Sakhana showed himself to the nearby captain,
who recognized and moved to embrace him.
Sakhana asked after Zoe's pursuers.
They had been here, the captain said,
and gone hence some time ago.
They had seen no one else.

Marius Nikolai brought word back to Zoe in the cave.
At once, she determined to see what became of her family.
Sakhana accompanied her to the top of the cliff.
Inside, the house was empty but for a message.

They had left in haste, their duty discharged:
to care for the changeling princess until
her identity should be discovered.
Zoe held the gem shard,
and knew what her pursuers were seeking.
Her kingdom was dead, not of this world,
so it was said by the dying man
who brought her as an infant to this cliffside.
He had given them her true name, Viridis Merida.
It was said that should she ever go to her old home,
it would be her doom. Zoe wept.
She knew she had seen it,
and that she could not go back there, nor stay.
Sakhana asked her to come with him
where he would rebuild his country.
Though grieving, she agreed to the journey.

Sakhana showed himself to the nearby captain,
who recognized and moved to embrace him.
Sakhana asked after Zoe's pursuers.
They had been here, the captain said,
and gone hence some time ago.
They had seen no one else.

Marius Nikolai brought word back to Zoe in the cave.
At once, she determined to see what became of her family.
Sakhana accompanied her to the top of the cliff.
Inside, the house was empty but for a message.

They had left in haste, their duty discharged:
to care for the changeling princess until
her identity should be discovered.
Zoe held the gem shard,
and knew what her pursuers were seeking.
Her kingdom was dead, not of this world,
so it was said by the dying man
who brought her as an infant to this cliffside.
He had given them her true name, Viridis Merida.
It was said that should she ever go to her old home,
it would be her doom. Zoe wept.
She knew she had seen it,
and that she could not go back there, nor stay.
Sakhana asked her to come with him
where he would rebuild his country.
Though grieving, she agreed to the journey.

Marius Nikolai and Viridis Merida
left with the trading vessel,
making many calls to port.
As they approached Old Babylon,
there was more rumor of what was lost
and gained in the fall of the city.
Some spoke of the Magus,
and how its last son was missing,
but Marius Nikolai kept his identity secret.

They arrived at the port of Babylon Magus
with an abundance of goods, carrying
timber, fiber, stone and food.
These he distributed among people,
still not revealing his identity.
Zoe went with him, healing and listening,
keeping the jewel concealed.
By its magic, she gained knowledge of ways to live
without the forces that corrupted the city
and brought its downfall. This she shared
with Sakhana and his people.
In time, they prospered.
The city as they knew it disappeared, brick by gear.

Boxes that looked like bricks and building debris were sent through the crowd, and opened to reveal gifts and treats. The well-dressed crowd between the Maray and the Diplomat's District were appreciative.

As the old fortress was being cleared,
Marius Nikolai found a cellar door he hadn't before seen,
blown askew on its hinges. A hallway led into the earth.
He journeyed in, bringing none but Viridis Merida,
who would not leave his side.

The hallway went to a bank of empty storerooms.
In the last of these, Sakhana found
a hidden trapdoor with a ladder going further down.
Here he entreated Zoe to turn back,
but she would not, so they went on together.
So absorbed were they in the mystery of this place,
they didn't see the torch running low
until it began to gutter.

They were enveloped by darkness, and fear arose.
Sakhana banished the angry spirits that crowded his mind.
As they made to turn back in trepidation,
Viridis Merida saw a glow in her pocket.

She withdrew the gem, and it lit the hall.
So they continued.

Before long, the passageway ended.
They examined the dusty end, uncertain.
As Zoe held the gem to the wall,
a light answered forth, describing a door
with its hidden mechanism.

The door was represented by a mechanical gate with lights along its moving parts. Counterweights and pulleys opened it for the actors behind.

Marius Nikolai and Viridis Merida
entered a vast library chamber.
The walls bearing volumes were flanked by
massive statues that glowed as though living.
These took many forms, that Sakhana recognized
as his people's ancient teachers of myth.
He bent a knee before them, and at the sight of this place.

Zoe held the jewel aloft, and
the library responded with its own illumination.
In wonder, they explored and examined the trove.
Many of the finest volumes were empty,
by myriad items of unknown but powerful magic.

A wall of books opened before Zoe
as she approached it holding the gem.
It revealed a stairway of masterful craft.
Upon the stone steps were carved tales of great heroes.
Sakhana asked Zoe if she would stay behind,
and again she refused.
So together they took the long, winding stair.

Here they passed the great military obelisk as the actors climbed illusory stairs. The projectionists displayed carved story reliefs in the surrounding space, making it look for a moment as though the stairs went all the way up the building.

When at last they reached light,
they found themselves atop Mt. Kairas.
Marius Nikolai had not known the place.
He found there a slender stone standing to chest height,
in the top of it a small window. The solstice sun set,
and the gem of Viridis Merida glowed again
with a piercing light that fell directly on the stone.
So she brought it close, placing it within the window.
The jewel pulsed, growing brighter each time.
Then with a deafening silence,
the light enveloped the entire city.

The parade arrived in the Royal Court. The bright display played off the walls of the city's most fantastical architecture, setting a backdrop for the arrival of Her Vast Eminence, Queen Celeste. She was brought to the royal platform where she boarded, below and in front of her second oldest granddaughter. They continued to the Verdant Plateau nearby. In the Pergola waited representatives from neighboring planets, and a Dragon.

All across the land could see it, near and far.
Within the encompassing veil of light shone visions,
sharp and clear, of a realm with more grace and triumph
than any they had seen.
Every detail of it etched into every looking eye.

Nor could any eye miss the man and woman
atop the mountain, revealed in majesty.
Though distant, their faces became known to all in that moment.

Marius Nikolai and Viridis Merida were recognized thus.
They stewarded the beginning of the next age of marvels,
and the new city that became Alisandre Capital.

So at Pyrean Midsummer we conjure forth our visions,
bright and clear as the light of Zoe's gem,
great and certain enough to lay the foundation
for our futures in the spirit of new hope.

To Marius Nikolai!
To Viridis Merida!
To Alisandre!
And to the Great Pan-Galactic Imperium!

A twenty-one person assembly waited atop the Verdant
Plateau – one dragon, four Aquarii, and sixteen humans
arrayed above, inside, and around the Pergola. The procession
halted at the plateau's edge, and alone the ruling family
disembarked to join them.

"This is the big show, Chrysanthe. The Vision. You were a
baby last time you saw this." The young girl, still just small

enough to ride atop her father's shoulders, squished his cheeks between her palms. They had a distant view from amid the sea of people filling the valley south of the Plateau. He kept her hands off his face by holding them. "Of course, it's never the same twice. But I remember you smiling."

"I doubt I could really see it if I was just a baby."

"Maybe so. It's good luck for you to be born so near Pyrean Midsummer. Now that you're seven you get to see why."

The Queen's voice rolled out over the surrounding valleys, transmitted into space beyond. "Now with all the peoples of the Imperium, we light the sky with the Pyrean Vision." The Magus family turned to face the great Pergola, and together sat on their knees.

"Papa – why do they kneel?"

"A show of respect for the hopes and dreams we express in the Vision."

The four Aquarii in their respective corners of the Pergola began to shimmer warmly. The four humans surrounding each Aquari raised their palms, and the light around the Aquarii grew. A deep, melodic thrumming pervaded the air as their spheres of light widened to intermingle, beaming through the open Pergola.

"See how the Aquarii channel the human representatives, mixing them all in one Rasakarya."

"What's a ross-corey again?"

"A synaesthetic, like multisensory, living portrait of emotion and thought. Something only Aquarii can do."

"How come those people get to do it?"

Chrysanthe's father took a deep breath, and laughed. "This event is unique, 'Santhe. Them up there are the ones that start it, but actually we all get to take part." At no response but silence, he checked to see his daughter's face transfixed by the spectacle.

Aural melodies began to wail, soar and syncopate. Intricate brightness enveloped the entire Pergola, reaching the coiled body of the dragon perched in massive flying form on the roof. Er silver-blue scales flashed as 'e took to the air, gently spiraling to float high above.

The mass of light gained focus, a streaming latticework that converged on a pulsing point centered above the structure. "It's all joined now, see, and they're making sense of it." Glowing geometry transformed through a series of iterations that became more concise and graceful. The central point grew brighter till it burst upward, illuminating the sky all the way to the dragon above.

"What dragon is that?"

"Let's see, that's not Arkuda..." He pulled the event program from his pocket. "That's Arctyri, of Foshan. Saga, Kyridi, and Rhizoa are on the other three planets this Midsummer." The young girl repeated the names quietly.

The light revealed the dragon's greater spectral being, extending through the sky in whorls and spikes. Arctyri's body navigated a toroidal pattern, bending and channeling the light in this shape. The color of the sky began to change.

"Now the dragons are uniting the Visions from across the universe, from four planets in four separate galaxies who share the same moment of summer solstice every seven years. Right now!"

"When do we get to join in?"

"You'll see. You'll know!" Chrysanthe held her father's hands and craned her head to watch. The sun was setting to her left. Between the growing night and fading day, the sky did resemble a conduit reaching through the universe; though instead of being dark, it was varicolor luminescent. She untangled a hand to reach up to it.

The combined light of four sunsets filled the air overhead, breathed in by the motion of the dragons' flight. The colors gained substance and weight, falling like mist until they reached upraised hands.

It wasn't like rain or snow, but Chrysanthe felt it, an electric sparkle that raised the hairs on her skin. It reminded her of things: warm cereal in the morning, dancing to the music her parents played. She saw the colors respond around her hand, and she did know just what to do after all. She tilted her head as the lines and figures issuing from her father's hand rose to meet her own small pictures. The expressions were abstracted, but when they joined, it somehow made a little more sense. Chrysanthe turned to see it happening everywhere around her. The sunsets' light was fading, and the grand picture grew brighter in turn. She could see lines now that didn't come from around her, but from somewhere across the galaxies, and they too connect into the picture with meaning. It seemed miles wide.

Arctyri above released the energy from the glowing torus, sending it back to the central focus. As a point of static harmony was reached, the Aquarii sent the energy crackling back through the pattern, rays of light connecting disparate lines.

When the big egg came falling through the vision like a springtime surprise, Chrysanthe wondered what amazing thing would come from inside.

} 64 {

"We have to wait. They're running emergency traffic signals, limiting in and out-bound. There's a newscast about it." Wendel Harper reached up to tune in the overhead speakers. The boy sitting copilot and the passenger hushed up to listen.

"The Pyrean Midsummer Vision was interrupted today by Raev Sturlusson, who descended from the skies on the capital during the final moments of the intergalactic solstice celebration. The capsule he descended in was emitting an agent bearing HA235, the disease that decimated the planet Hirylien twenty-five years ago. Many attendees are already experiencing symptoms. The Verdant Plateau of Alisandre Capital is under quarantine, and vision attendants are being held there and at Eldea Hospital." As this narrated, they silently turned to meet each other's eyes.

Hydraia rose from the fold-down seat to stand behind the pilot's chairs. "We're waiting to be let in to the main transport arena, correct?"

Harper nodded. "That's right. They've paged us with a wait time of a couple hours, but there's no telling how long we'll be in line." She pointed to a timer on the air traffic display.

The passenger pulled a piece of paper from her pocket. "Here. Establish a link with this frequency." Harper checked it and nodded.

After a short moment, someone answered. "Spear Traffic Control, how can I assist you?" At mention of the capital's towering military building, the captain faced her passenger in mute surprise.

"This is Drt. Arcta Hydraia of the Loramer Institute, requesting entry to the Helianth Airlot."

"Acknowledged Drt. Hydraia, do you have a clearance code?"

"2-10-6-P-Night-C3W."

"Thank you, Doctorate. Drift 9, new traffic directions have been sent. You may proceed."

65

King Ascendant Grant Vario raised the mask to his face and activated it. The hairs on his arm lifted as the ion barrier activated around him, effecting a blue glow. He nodded to the Dragon Councillor, and they exited the transport onto the grounds of Eldea Hospital, accompanied by a security escort.

The quarantine guards opened the door for them. Inside, the halls were filled with people reacting to their symptoms, rubbing their faces and blinking. Back when the sickness appeared on the planet Hirylien, there had been no knowledgeable measures. By the time they recognized the epidemic, the majority of the planet had been infected. The symptoms had been difficult to distinguish until they were too serious for any recovery, and no counteragent had been discovered. This time, they'd recognized it almost immediately.

From the room she shared with her father and two other patients, Chrysanthe watched the hallway. The retinue walked past, and she saw the second dragon she'd ever seen in her life. Arkuda's scaly form gleamed next to the King Ascendant's grave face, and they passed in a quick moment before she could mention it. She wasn't sure if her sight had already gotten fuzzy, like they told her it would, or if they were really glowing. She turned her head and succumbed to drowsiness, closing her eyes on the sight of her sleeping father.

They met with the head of the hospital, who debriefed them on the patient population. Those furthest along were beginning to lose their eyesight to nerve degeneration. Vario took this in, but refrained comment.

They passed through layers of security till Arkuda and the King Ascendant were outside Sturlusson's room. The guard coded them in.

Inside, the quarantine prisoner sat shirtless in the bedside chair. Hospital equipment had all been moved to the corner. At the sight of visitors, he rose to his feet. "I am honored. The King Ascendant, and his dragon." Arkuda gazed at him in silence.

Vario faced him squarely, hands behind his back. "You declined treatment, even though you tested positive for HA235."

"Yes."

"So is this, then, your farewell note to the Imperium?"

Framed by his dark hair, a smile crossed his face. "No." He locked gaze on the King Ascendant as he sat down again.

Arkuda eyed Raev Sturlusson sidelong. Over the man's collection of tattoos, 'e glimpsed disruption patterns invisible to human eyes. Residue of communication with others. The dragon studied him intently.

Vario clasped his hands tightly. "We have reports now of cases on Ionos and Lurin. How many more outbreaks are we to expect?"

"How many more do you need in order to put an end to them?" Arkuda watched his surrounding disruption evaporate.

The King Ascendant drew himself up. "We are now enacting the same quarantines that we did on your home planet. You were lucky to have survived."

"I really was." The communicative traces reappeared as Sturlusson joined together different faces of his fingers. He looked at them through half-closed eyes. Arkuda stirred the air toward the prisoner with er breath, observing the patterns reacting.

King Ascendant Vario made a prompt and wordless exit. Sturlusson angled his hand sign to the dragon Councillor, who curled a lip before exiting in turn.

} 66 {

The airlot manager stood with Arcta Hydraia and Wendel Harper by the Drift 9, surrounded by military and council vehicles. The wind was high, and they raised their voices to speak over it.

"Ms. Harper. I'm required to use private transport during my consult with the Spear. I'll be traveling between here and the Libran Federet. Are you available exclusively for the short term?"

Wendel tilted her head and nodded. She'd been half expecting the offer. Setting herself on an appointed route might be a good way to let trouble blow over. She jerked her elbow toward the ship. "What about the boy?"

The airlot manager considered. "We may be able to offer him clearance."

"I'll be here for the night," said Hydraia. "I'll get in touch with you soon, if you want to talk it over with him." The captain shook hands with Hydraia, waving as she re-entered the ship.

She set herself back down in her chair. From where he remained in his seat, Toller looked past the airlot shadows toward the Royal Court. "Dr. Hydraia is hiring me up for a shuttle route. You can probably stay with me so long as you'll be handy."

Toller lifted a hand at the view. "We're at the capital now."

Wendel smiled, remembering he'd never seen this before. "Yeah. Old Alisandre." Her gaze traveled up the dark octagonal obelisk to the sky.

Toller tapped his teeth together in consideration. "Tell you what," said Wendel, powering her ship. "We'll decide over dinner."

} 67 {

In a waiting chamber in a middle floor of the Spear, the dragon Councillor and er protege sat kneeling against one wall. The Scion Princess' eyes searched the patterned tapestry facing them. The dragon opened er eyes.

"The man you're going to see - I observed points of contact on him. Communication disturbance, perhaps. I recognized patterns there, and I feel troubled about it. So be aware, in every way." She breathed deeply, returning er look. 'E nodded and rose to exit the room.

The Princess rested alone until the door opened once more, and her father stepped inside. "If you're ready, Soleil." She stood and straightened herself, inclining her chin before joining him.

They walked down the hallway past two corner turns. The walls of the octagonal tower turned gently around them, regularly giving way to heavy framed windows.

"You've been made aware of the state of things at the Verdant Plateau and in the quarantine areas, and of the other new outbreaks. You've heard what he's done over the last twenty years, so you have some idea of who we're encountering.

"We're fortunate in not having contracted the affliction. Though tests show that Sturlusson has HA235, he's not developing symptoms. We're not taking chances, so," he passed her a barrier field mask, "here you are. Observe him well, Soleil. He'll soon be on trial. That's why he's here now." They donned their masks outside the guarded door, engaging the minute blue glow before they went in.

The prisoner sat on the floor, his back against a wall bench. At their entry, he rose to his feet. Soleil walked in behind her father. The man before her was not as he looked in projections. The air around him roiled with energy, and she stayed on guard.

The King Ascendant gestured to the wall benches, and they all sat; the Scion Princess and her father on one side, Sturlusson on the other. "Ionos," began Vario. "We found your agent there, one Teryj Lakos. From Hirylien, like you. He's told us enough to find the rest. But we know there's more. Where?"

A grin spread across Raev Sturlusson's face. For a moment, the Princess' vision grew dark, and her temples felt warm.

"Waiting, aren't they." Her voice sounded thunderous hearing it for the first time since she woke. Sturlusson raised his eyebrows. King Ascendant Vario turned to regard her.

7th
sequence

} 68 {

Bright Wave sat curled at the base of the tree growing from the platform over the valley below. With half-closed eyes, she moved a line of color across the sunset. Slowly, and with care – previous ambitious attempts at expression had made her faint.

Her reverie was interrupted by the big grey pietrobird, scattering rocks as it landed. She rose from her seat, and went to look the bird eye to eye where it stood. It hopped backward, pealing loudly, and dropped below the ledge before its eyes popped over again. Someone may be down in the mountain. She sent the bird a flash of color, which it spread its wings to absorb.

Bright Wave moved down the rock face. Halfway down, outside the cave, hovered a vehicle. With a tentacle she parted the vine curtain to see a mantled Fleeting Shade.

They stepped toward each other, tendrils lifting. They met partway, super and subsonic vibrations popping in the air. The leaves on the vines shook lightly.

Lead Composer Fleeting Shade gestured, and a stage floor shimmered in to surround them. Figures in red and white danced around the edges. The star image above reflected a specific sky in two weeks' time.

Bright Wave cast her tentacles aside and whipped one around in a circle, marring the picture with scratches. She would have dispelled it entirely, but it remained. Her supersonics morphed to echo the burning Symbias, which made him flinch. She reached out to him again, and the dead silence of the groves fell around them. She sagged, her head hanging.

Fleeting Shade held her up, and the edges of the stage surrounded the silence. The figures in red and white appeared, drawing themselves into the dead space around them. They had eyes, and ears.

She straightened and looked up. Before her she created a candlepoint of light, which grew to the size of her head, then faded. She tried again to make it brighter, but couldn't, tendrils shaking in frustration. He drew her in to hold her. The stage and people remained.

69

From her perspective in darkness, the occasional sound reached her ears. Chrysanthe was thinking of her pillow and blanket forts – the way everything became dark and hot, smelling of her own breath, and she listened to her father in the house. She couldn't hear much more, so she stayed in that cozy place.

Her dad hadn't said anything since she'd last slept, but he was nearby. When she reached for him, he played with her hand a little. The occasional squeeze was enough to reassure her, since she didn't know if he couldn't speak, or she just couldn't hear him.

People approached, talking. Just the rise and fall of their voices, through many layers. She jiggled his hand and he wiggled back.

"We've sent so many nurses to other planets. Thank you for volunteering."

"This seemed an appropriate time to step back in. Yet, I've never done triage. What am I looking for?"

"This is our first sweep. We're reaction testing. This device measures muscular nerve response and blood flow to extremities. There's a threshold." She showed the readout to the volunteer. "During high rush, patients below that will have lowest priority as instructed. I'll show you." She gestured to the man holding his daughter's hand. "He's awake, we'll start with him." The nurse cradled his other hand in hers and he flexed it. He did the same for Chrysanthe on the other side. The voices were louder to the little girl, going wah wahh wahhh.

The nurse put the holding device in his hand and wrapped his fingers around it, squeezing them. She released and cradled it for a moment until the device light turned color. She checked it, and glanced at the other patients around the room before showing it to the volunteer aide. "This is a significant reading, below threshold by a margin. Input the command here, and his bracelet will carry the tag. And that's it."

The aide nodded. "I'll watch while you check the next patient over here."

} 70 {

"Due to energy pattern expansion rates, we need to widen flight paths beyond the C sphere, here." With her laser pen she colored the zone orange.

"Except for you people," Arcta indicated the technical instrument pilots, "because you're carrying the Dyson probes and photon sounders. You're in two teams, each covering a hemisphere. There is a set rotation plan, in case communication equipment is affected. We already have some signal bandwidth workarounds."

The door opened, and General Iparia stepped in. Dr. Hydraia straightened.

"Now for those of you shadow marking – priority observations are signal strength, signal length, placement, and finally type."

"Don't you think the subject of what we see might be more important than the quantified signatures?"

Arcta looked down and let half a smile emerge. "Those of you who've examined the list of signal types have found, I'm sure, that the list keeps growing longer and is already too long to memorize. Type recognition is last priority because attempting it would keep attention from every other reading. The data is being pored over at Loramer. If they find a useful pattern in it, then we might shift our focus there. Until then, let's concern ourselves with the possible effects and direction of the energy output, and how to handle and defend ourselves from it."

Iparia leaned against the wall, arms crossed.

"And we'll detach one team – that's you – to array themselves between here and Photuris. You'll have a more sensitive set of instruments. We want you to sit there, and read. I'm sorry we can't just deploy satellites for this – we want people there live reading, and able to respond."

"That's all you need to hear from me. Your officers will give you the nitty gritty." She watched the pilots exit, saluting the General as they passed. Hydraia cleared her data display.

The General took a step forward. "We're going to assign two shadow markers to type cataloguing."

"That would leave holes in our coverage. We've already thinned out in order to create a buffer zone."

"I think the greater hole in our knowledge would be to ignore this information. We can spare that much, so that's what we'll do."

"Do you realize that the energy dynamic in that sphere is over twenty times that of any known anomaly? And we still have no reason, or insight other than confusion. Diverting resources from safety on something practically pointless is reckless. I hope you understand that."

"That's what we'll do until or unless we can bring out another Alpha base."

At this point Hydraia nodded, turning around to put things in her bag. "I'm heading to Alpha 1, and back in three days." On her way out she stopped to salute. "General."

She crossed the corridors of the Alpha base to where the Drift 9 was docked. Arcta entered straight to the cockpit where Wendel Harper lounged in the captain's chair. She chucked her stuff into a bin and flopped down next to her, heaving a sigh. "Fools. They really have no idea."

Wendel straightened and began powering the ship. "That kind of day today?"

} 71 {

"I'm being transferred to Ionos. They'll put me on show shortly. There's nothing you wouldn't already know."

"Your sham trial is not a concern. We can feel them meddling with the relay amplifier. Are you ensuring they are properly misdirected?"

"Someone's making sure they're properly misdirecting themselves. They wouldn't recognize the technology for some time anyhow, given their own devices. The Imperium may have picked up some Vedani trash, but the cutting edge, combined with your additions, is outside their scope. The best researchers on the subject are currently occupied with other things. Is the power accrual going smoothly?"

"Certainly. Nothing is interfering with the core, which will soon be drained."

"Which is... devastating. I hear the survival rate has been very good."

"We've given them plenty of time where we could. But forces operate as they must."

"That's good to know."

} 72 {

Mireille loaded her bowl with greens as Margeaux took her seat.

"Glad you could join us, dear," Charlotte intoned, leaning forward to fill Margeaux's glass.

"My pleasure. Where is Queen Celeste?" she asked, looking around.

"The Queen pardoned herself for other matters," replied Vario. Mireille rotated the greens to Margeaux's place and dipped into the capers and onions.

Charlotte smiled, and asked "Have you spoken with Soleil in the last couple days?"

"Yeah!" Margeaux flashed a grin and laughed. "What a relief it is. I expected her to sound croaky, but it's her very same voice, only a little quiet." Charlotte nodded.

Mireille sampled her melange. "She hasn't been eating with us," she shrugged, "so."

Charlotte pressed her lips shut and looked at her husband. "It was a surprise, yes," said Vario. "One that I was glad to see. I was only expecting she would learn from the encounter as necessary, but her speech at that moment was revelatory."

"Can't argue with that," said Mireille. She tipped a ramekin of honeygrub dressing over her bowl and cracked pepper over it. Everyone continued to help themselves.

"It had been a while since we two caught a sunset together." Margeaux smiled as she nibbled.

"Here's to many more," toasted Charlotte, raising her glass. Vario returned the gesture, and the girls followed suit.

} **73** {

The panoramic door drew upward, revealing row after row of hard gazes landing squarely on the prisoner and his two keepers. The clamoring hiss fell silent. The three traveled up the center aisle toward the hearing platform ahead. From within the green-tinted keeper's field, Sturlusson received their suppressed snarls. He looked up at the ceiling full of recording lights, the fixated heads around him, and the arbiter's tiers beyond the rest. Passing the front row of assembly seats was like breaking a runner's tape.

At the pause before the platform, he was greeted by the three judges, and the King and Queen Ascendant above them. They all went through the requisite gestures. He eyed the empty witness' stand, and opposite that, to the right of the arbiter's tiers, the large screen where the Queen's face watched the proceedings.

As he stepped to the platform and the keepers attached the field to it, he felt nudges at the tip of either shoulder over his burn scars. Sturlusson glanced up again, and behind his field of vision he pinpointed two watching presences. Their communication with him was more or less clear.

"I loathe them, and watch this only under duress."

"I sort of know what you mean." He looked to the medallion above the tiers, which read Justice Is Served In Many Ways.

"Over the next few days, we will hear from witnesses who will present accounts of your doings. There are many in this hall who have waited some time for the opportunity, though their statements must remain brief, as must your rebuttals. You've opted against the presence of a legal interpreter, so you are responsible for adhering to the guidelines of reply."

He received a veiled stare from King Ascendant Vario in his red arbiter's garb as he paused his speech.

"From the witnesses' statements and your replies, we will build and subsequently examine the case to determine your sentence. For all that you yourself have taken credit for, you can expect no less than a great period of suffering." At this, Raev Sturlusson blinked slowly. He heard a hissing chuckle of irony.

} 74 {

It was like flipping through a yearbook, or being at a royal roast, or attending his own funeral. A little like all three. It was serious – every one would draw blood if allowed, but Raev remembered them more clearly than suspected. His past decisions were walking up to greet him, and he knew them very well.

The critical ones, everybody knew about. It started a long time ago, and he learned quickly how to use notoriety to his advantage. Some in particular created a lot of requisite damage, that he wished weren't so even as he made it happen. It was pointless telling them he didn't have horns – after all, he wore them so well. True, for some time his thirst for retribution could hardly be slaked. But it had taken him all those years to figure out why.

When he acquired that first gargantuan sum of funds off the Oligarchy of Tamakopa, it was enough to shut down companies and end towns. He'd known who would greet the citizens beyond the town borders, and now he learned how life had treated them. Ultimately well, he thought, but he must be held accountable.

There was the one he hated to hear, even though he reminded himself of it all the time. When he didn't keep her – lost her and everything in one fell swoop, all involved. People had never been more angry with him, and he with himself. Here he paid probably his greatest price.

After that was a lot of boat rocking, and sinkholing. And of course, the disappearance at the prestige. His return still had people fuming, most especially because he had won sympathy, and families divided over it.

Certain attributed tidbits, he did not recognize. He didn't bother making contest, only took in the news as it came to him. The source of his privately connected counsel noted the new information as well.

"They have added to your reputation."

"Clearly. Though I don't mind, as the time for setting things straight is not now. The tall tales are an added layer of distraction, which is fine with me. The truth overshadows them regardless, which is why they slip right in."

"How will they hang you for your current move?"

"They can't yet. However this centershow works out, they still need me to get them out of the corner. The King Ascendant and Queen haven't released a reverse agent. We got it from them after all, though we improved on it. I suspect what final option they're narrowing down to as far as handling this. I don't think I'm prepared to play lab rat to satisfy the cameras. They have days before a toll begins to mount, as far as they know." This final indictment was difficult, as its inconclusive nature brought everyone to edge.

Raev Sturlusson heard it all again in the Queen Ascendant's voice as she announced the collected statements.

8th SEQUENCE

} 75 {

The sphere image was frozen steady, drawn lines within reading as chaos. At one side of the table, the two Alpha Captains and General Ionos leaned forward. The General lifted a hand to the display. "Explain how the surrounding technicians are supposed to align and co-triangulate."

"My Loramer co-fellow can answer that," said Dr. Hydraia, turning to look at her colleague to the left.

"This is an unusual problem," said Arys Steinman, laying out a few notes. "We can create a system that will co-map a series of points, call them mirrors. For the interruption sequence we want to enact, each point needs to be an intersection of the signal figures we reviewed."

Steinman laid out the factor maps, pointing things out. "A technology pattern found in our Zerite-based inventions. The energy signature of an Iljen Engine at pre-critical burst. Here's the map of microhole readings, and shadow radius sectors.

"Each mirror spins at a live rate responding to the weather of the vortex, tethering to each technician ship along designated connection paths. Setting a mirror takes more energy input from the initiating technician until it can tether down multiple paths. You're tethering the mirrors, not the other way around.

"At a designated level of synergy, the energy to maintain the mirrornet will drop greatly. At this point, co-triangulation can run automatically, and we can move on to the next phase, precise insertion of chain reactives."

General Ionos sat back, looking partially satisfied. "You've said we do this rarely in application. What makes you confident that this maneuver will work at this scale, with live pilots instead of robotics?"

"We're keeping in mind that pre-critical burst phase of an Iljen Engine is only inwardly unstable. So while ships must remain in place to enact the interruption, they remain outside the boundary of collapse. In recorded failures, backlash occurred in the programming, preventing recurrence of the process without damaging equipment. The program you'll be using is contained separately from ship operations."

"How many times did you run this in simulation, and on how many levels? And did you do your utmost to minimize the number of technicians required?"

Arcta took in a slow breath. "We forwarded the ultimate simulations to you and your captains. If you want the complete logs, I can request them from Loramer Ultra sim rooms, but they were combed deeply and to do so again would be a great waste of time."

The General leaned on the table. "If we determine this course of action, when will we need to mobilize?"

"In about twelve days, we'll get our next likely shot in the vortex activity cycles."

} 76 {

The King Ascendant with his two armed guards filled the room when they entered. "Now that the verdict is being processed, we can attend to other pressing matters. The HA235 patients on Alisandre are nearing critical status, and thousands of people on three other planets are close behind them. Tell us everything now, because if they die, you will die with them."

"Wasn't I supposed to in the first place, with my family and home? Your stance and bluster don't convince me. You've held out far longer than I have with the truth of the matter, and not even the impending death of thousands will change your tune. If you want to keep all these people from dying, that's within your power. These deaths will dig your grave if you allow them."

"How are you carrying the disease and not suffering symptoms?" At his gesture, the guards flanked the prisoner.

"Have your doctors not figured that out, with the samples they took?"

Looking him in the eye, the King Ascendant stepped close. "They have not. But I believe the answer is in you, somewhere."

"It would have to be." Raev bowed his head for a moment before looking up at the three surrounding him. "You might be surprised how simple it is. Since the verdict is being processed, and I'm facing my fate, perhaps you deserve a farewell letter after all. Bring the doctor." He turned his right side to Vario and lifted his sleeve, revealing designs on his skin. "It's here. Beneath the winged horse in the lightning."

"Take off his arm." A guard drew a hot sword and it was gone. Raev Sturlusson sank to one knee. The King Ascendant picked up the limb, lifting the tattoo to his eyes. "Make sure he doesn't die." He exited, leaving the door open, blood decorating the hallway floor.

No sight or sound, given up trying to hear herself. She could feel her motions though, and the occasional shift let her know she was alive.

She thought in litanies, things to remember and wake up to, going in circles and ladders. It was hard not to fill the silence. Sometimes she just listened to it. She was breathing, even if she could no longer hear it.

A touch, coolness. Then, a pinprick.

She began to hear a sound - unfamiliar and far away, though comforting like a net in the void.

Language grew steadily louder. Had they taken her somewhere? She clenched her fists on occasion. It felt good.

It was a long time building. Occasionally, in her breath she felt a blast of fresh air.

Almost suddenly, she saw a bright triangle. She couldn't tell if it was big or small, it was just the only thing. As she thought about it, still itself it became a message.

Cousins... she learned where they found this disease. The planet who suffered by it, gone Hirylien. How they changed it, she would be okay, and why. She couldn't always keep her focus on it, but when she did, she learned a little more. It was fully understandable. She hung on to the net.

} 78 {

"I received some of your recent news broadcasts, and saw the King Ascendant waving your arm around. I admit to some amusement. You must have pushed him far."

"Oh, hardly at all. He didn't need much help."

"Are you surviving it well?"

"Other than painful attempts at using an arm that isn't there, I'm in good health. They gave me rush treatment to be sure I'd be well enough to receive my verdict."

"You sound fine, and it's good that you're healthy. The time is upon us."

"My elements are in place. There's no reason to change any part of the arrangement. Go forward without hesitation."

"What about the scion?"

"Her spirits have improved, even if her confusion has grown. I think she'll be coming to more specific understandings shortly."

"This could go different ways. People may prefer your version. We hope your plans hatch properly."

Sturlusson felt the contact dissipate. The door of his room opened quietly, and he raised his eyebrows. In came the girl, slipping in sideways. She closed the door and paused by the wall, appraising his condition with a grimace. He lay back in a hospital recliner, right shoulder heavily swaddled. Soleil could detect a smile beneath his unwavering gaze. She took a deep breath, blinking.

He dipped his head. "Your Grace the Scion Princess."

She stepped toward him with a controlled voice. "You were in my vision during my coma sleep. Who are you and and what are you doing here? Why couldn't I speak until I saw you?"

He stretched his head back to gaze at the cieling. "Not much I can tell you, Scion Princess, that would give you greater insight." Around his neck and face a roiling shimmer

formed. Soleil stepped backward, and Raev Sturlusson met
her eyes without moving.

A consistent swirl formed between them. Soleil looked into
it, and clapped her hands over her eyes. She staggered a little,
but kept them there, breathing. The volcanic earthquakes of
Genesee filled her sight, and she zipped through a whirlwind
of relays - the Aquari Home Fires, portals bursting with
newly familiar presences, and depthless chasms emptying in
conflagration. She tore her hands from her eyes and looked
over at the prisoner with dread.

She went to the door, looking silently back at Raev
Sturlusson one more time before she left.

} 79 {

The gentleman tugged at his collar as he looked out over
the floor, then to his friend. "Thank you for dragging me out.
Would have been a shame to miss it. So, who is this year's
beneficiary for the Claret Occasion?"

"The Genesee Refugee Fund."

"Oh, what about Aquari Home Recovery?"

"Well you see, there are still lives to be saved on Genesee. With five new red zones, we have to practically depopulate the planet, which you can imagine takes time. We haven't depopulated anywhere since Hirylien, which - had pretty much happened already." He sipped from his wine glass. "And not for generations before that. Geologists have gone from stumped to overwhelmed in their attempts at prediction. So, crisis before recovery."

"I understand that." The gentleman inhaled sharply. "Bright Wave's up to perform, isn't she? I'm glad she's well enough to do the occasion this year."

His friend with the white ruffled collar nodded. "Her performances are a pleasure and a privelege."

The two wandered from the upper tier where they'd left silent auction bids, nodding to others passing by in red and white. They refilled their cups at a lower tier, and made their way up an aisle to take seats. Below on the floor in the center, dancers were finishing the Mobius Spiral to the sound of a brass ensemble. Applause rose at the end as people filtered up the slopes and steps.

An oval of light burst into glow on the now cleared floor, and the plane within elevated, revealing the lifting stage walls and spiral staircase. The double doors in the side were revealed, and parted.

An Aquari man emerged and placed himself atop the stage, facing in. "That's a Lead Composer."

"That's THE Lead Composer. She brought a Sendsinger?" They looked at each other.

Fleeting Shade folded his legs to kneel. The amphitheater had gone quiet, but for a deep bass wave washing in like breath. The place turned dim but for a glow remaining at the door. She emerged shrouded in mist, moving by her tentacles and tendrils, carapace trailing behind her. Up the stairs her body rolled, the mist growing as it mingled with the bass in ripples. Bright Wave curled crouching opposite the Sendsinger, facing in.

From where she stayed, she moved a figure around in the mist like a shadow. The bass rose to the beat of a resounding wall. Flashes revealed columns like a maze for the figure to weave through as it grew with the sound.

It wove its way to the center, where it rested against something bright. The mist clarified into luminous points. More Aquarii came through the door and up, to crouch around the edge, facing out. There were eight, and their echoing sounds only occasionally overlapped.

In a hollow, windy voice Bright Wave spoke a two-note phrase, and the bright something in the center showed color. She did it again, and so did another of the crouching Aquarii.

Again and again the relay echo grew, until the pulse moved continuously.

The central figure gripped the bright something, pulling itself up. All of them rose. The pulse changed, and the points of light expanded to fill the entire amphitheater. The music turned clear and loud.

The gentleman watching from the seats waved his finger to encircle the performers. "Those are all Sendsingers."

"Yes, indeed."

Then the language began. It was amusing! No one had any idea what they were saying, but it was certainly funny. As people around the amphiteater laughed, that became the central chorus of the music.

Sun rose, shining on the bright something. Its light condensed into a swirling trunk, the glow branching upward and spreading out. One by one, the eight Sendsingers visited. It pulsed and sang differently for each; and as they walked away, so too did they sing differently. All eight returned to sit around it together. The pulse continued as they watched the branching light, their gathered music illustrated above it.

The door glowed again, and eight more Sendsingers walked in to fill the places around the stage, facing out.

The gentleman swirled his finger at this in maddening circles. "Are all of them?"

His friend looked agog. "Well, yes. And that must be nearly half of them." He gripped his armrests and looked behind him as though he could see the sky. "How is traffic running right now?" He noticed other audience members in discreet communication. He sank back into his seat a little.

The cloud above reflected those sitting beneath. A color portal engulfed the trunk and branches, reaching the ground. Bright Wave rose and walked into the center of it, and it became a swirling mirror with sides. The inside eight rose together and stepped through.

In the amphitheater, the atmosphere changed. It seemed any point could lead to any other. These pathways became traveled, by few and then by many. If people touched them, they changed. The eight who stepped through found one of the eight around the edge. They sat back to back and twined their tentacles, one facing in, the other facing out. The pathways extended beyond the amphitheater.

In the center Bright Wave sat, leaning against the tree, which was there. She reached up to touch the billowing sheets of motion, twined and hanging from the branches. Great gusts flowed inward through the Sendsingers, to the branches and trunk where Bright Wave could touch them, and she weaved. The air was full of clear Aquari melodies from eight different kinds of far away.

"Could this be live?" he asked, holding down his white ruffles. At the word live, an unseen group of Aquarii echoed the word in confirmation. Live. He gasped, and his was not the only one.

The Sendsingers began switching pairs, counter-rotating. Human voices became a loud addition, and the sound of a dragon.

From a vantage point in the city, Toller watched the amphitheater surrounded in glowing whorls. If he cocked an ear, he could even hear it. His chuckle seemed to fit right in with the music.

Then something broke. It was wrong immediately. People could no longer hear their voices correctly, and when they grabbed for the threads, they weren't there. It was the frantic feeling of something important missing. The bright branches fell apart and floated away. The Sendsinger's channels fluttered. The trunk disappeared, down to the ground until there was only a heap in which Bright Wave sat. The weaving in her hands threatened to disappear, but she sent ends of it to the Aquarii surrounding her. They held to it as though suspended. The points in the sky reappeared above them.

Something is happening on the outskirts that the Imperium isn't prepared for - but we're responsible for it. And it wasn't my mother, or father, or grandmother who informed me, but them. I don't quite understand who they are - except for him, that one - which feels like the greater part of the problem.

Tonight is the yearly Claret Occasion, which I'm not required to attend, though I'll likely be missed. Instead I've contracted transport to Alisandre's outer orbit, where I'm going to peer through the scope array. Both the new ones through which I can view every one of the Imperium's planets, and the old ones that helped us find these distant galaxies in the first place.

9th
SEQUENCE

} 81 {

The Array Synthesis room was clean and empty for her when she arrived, all consoles running as she requested. Soleil knew where she wanted to look, a set of coordinates based on her impression of its whereabouts.

She stepped into the suspension chair and engaged the full harness. It lifted, giving her the 47-million-degree view. She opened out the banks of physical adjustors and eyepiece optics, calling them within reach. The picture in her mind was like a child's drawing – the fewer obfuscating details, the better.

The pre-Ricardian scopes featured many degrees of diffraction, and she took a moment to enjoy the antique view that was a revelation to the seekers. She twiddled it, and looked into the scatter dimension. She shook her head at the moment she felt like an ancestor, as though she were looking through someone else's eyes, back in her line. There was something nebulous that the micrometers wouldn't pick up, something parallax that current technology ruled out.

Hints at details were aligning, and she moved on to fine tuning. There was a seam stretched far and wide, and she was finding the stitches. She had seen it all next to each other as though it were one thing that faced out in many directions.

The directions that she recognized weren't near each other at all, but she didn't worry about it – just kept finding them when things looked right, as she'd seen them there one after the other. The picture wasn't complete, but it should be enough.

She collected all the views, superimposing and shuffling till she saw it there. Not a hole. Maybe a bump. She stretched and collapsed them together like a deck of cards. Yeah, it was there. She paused at this.

The contact through her coma wasn't just an introduction. There was a deep history arriving to be accounted for, and Soleil understood why it was she who'd been called to task. When she went to see the hated criminal by her own devices, he'd given her a glimpse of things happening now, all at once, many and strong, everywhere and incomprehensible. So she worked with every impression.

In her notebook were drawings from the symbols, images, views, and her deductions. She translated these into coordinates, locations, directions, distances. She looked at the notebook nearby, being read in midair. The room was orbit station quiet as she hovered two feet over the ground.

The Princess readdressed the set of astronomical pinpoints, and drew a connecting line. She reordered them by proximity, tiling them by their signal sightlines in a triangular mesh. She set mirrors, and sent a signal loop from the corner that would touch every point in turn before repeating, and waited.

The remaining presence in her thoughts (confirmed when she saw Sturlusson) which made possible her glimpse into imminence, was still there. She'd gained some understanding of it, the cup on a string hanging in the corner. She picked it up and listened, hoping the dots were connected.

The mirrors began to miss. They didn't hit their spot or return correctly. The signal returned stronger, and she realized she was the mirror.

A rectangular dark patch opened in the space before her, bright motes flashing across it. A murmur of speech infiltrated her hearing.

"We see you again. Now you're awake."

"I don't fully understand what I've found here, but I want to know more. I have questions about the things I've seen. You seem very much like us, though your allies are stranger."

"We recognize your desire for understanding. There is much to be explained, and we are willing to share education. But these are matters both heavy and delicate, and it would not be a short amount of time."

"I will take all the time it requires. This is my priority."

The dark patch deepened, the motes flashing brighter. "We can bring you through, if you are so prepared. We desire your presence."

Soleil gestured for the program to set her notebook down on a panel. "I seek resolution from all this information. Where would you bring me?"

"Out of the world you know, that's for certain." The motes gathered themselves into a glowing ball, which floated towards her. "When you are ready, you can take the sphere."

The Scion Princess disengaged herself from the floating harness and loosened her joints. She took a soft look back at the view of Alisandre before lifting her hand to the glowing light. A bright net encased her, the dark patch enfolded her, and the Array Synthesis room was empty but for her few belongings.

} 82 {

"Then they got me involved, and I kind of told them that you exist. So they're probably coming at you with a job offer. I hope I haven't done anything too terrible and that you'll forgive me. Maybe this will be fun."

Derringer bit his lip and shook his head as he followed his guide, who had not once looked at him since he arrived. He laid one considering footstep after the other. From his years of experience, he was wary of of official jobs – if you couldn't fill the bill, they had a way of taking it out of you. But this seemed like a good way to get swept up, and besides he might be getting overfond of that lady. Must be mutual, if she put the big dogs on his tail. So here he was, walking straight into the Spear.

As the guard stopped in front of the office door, Derringer checked if there was anything he needed to remember before walking in. The door opened, and he went in remembering nothing.

He faced a desk with a placard that read General Alisandre, Draig Claymore. The man behind it had a stack of papers on either side, signing them as they moved from one end to the other. "Welcome," he said, "and thank you for never having been here."

"It's an honor." He took the other seat at the General's gesture.

"I value your credentials, and those who gave them to me." General Alisandre signed another paper carefully. "It's my duty to explore every possible avenue in my search, and I hope you can help me. Do you have any idea what I'm asking you to find?"

"An important person may be missing."

The General nodded. "Official channels are already engaged, and we have scant days before it becomes a matter of public knowledge. Can you work under that kind of scrutiny?"

"Sure, especially if that's not really what I'm doing."

"No, of course not. Your actual employment would of course be your own business. And you would have all means at your disposal to accomplish it."

"Means are helpful, so long as they're not under supervision."

"Why would they be? You're not connected to anyone in this building."

"Sounds like business as usual."

"You will remain completely independent. We simply wish for the goal to be accomplished."

"I think I can set myself to business as usual with a goal in mind."

"Remember, we have no idea what it is you're supposed to be doing."

"Who does?"

The General signed one more paper, and put away his pen. "I'm having beef and beer for lunch. Perhaps you'd like to join me on the terrace?"

"There's a terrace?"

"Oh yes, it's lovely. And there's more than one." They stood, and exited to an empty hallway.

} 83 {

Queen Ascendant Charlotte stood facing the green-haired researcher in a chamber to themselves.

"Thank you for being willing to speak with me so directly, Your Grace."

"Not at all. My priorities are clear, as parent and Ascendant. So, tell me about the surprise findings. I am up to date on the rest of the information regarding the Photuris Anomaly."

Hydraia nodded. "I first noticed it while idly searching the shadow visual classifications. Patterns or formations will pop out variously, as this did. It struck me as both eerie and timely. I even sent it to Loramer for a second opinion, and they agreed. It looks like a picture of your daughter."

The news had already been broken to the elder woman, so she took it well, reaching out to accept a copy of the data report. A pieced together image played above it: Soleil, looking over her shoulder.

The Queen Ascendant breathed deeply, looking intensely at the woman. "I realize your waking hours may be fully occupied, but I have need of some of them."

Arcta acknowledged this with a nod. "I sent the matter to your attention thinking you might act on it."

"My intentions are already forming, but I will need some dedicated, available guidance."

"There is currently no one who can fill my role on Alphas 1 and 2 in the Photuris Sector. But I can be interrupted under prominent need."

"Then I shall supply you with a communication line. I will not aim to make any interruptions. Just for burning questions."

"Your Grace, I extend my correct sympathy, and I wish to offer as much of my time as you require."

"You've already given us our first real discovery in the matter. We have four days before you are to enact a collapse interruption, right?" Queen Ascendant Charlotte finally offered her visitor a seat.

} 84 {

"Hey, what's shaking you guys." The redheaded dulcet tone spoke from disembodied audio. "How's the office working out for you?"

"Good. We've been making cash credit under our new company name: Substitute Security & Systems. We'll jack you up and make sure you don't get jacked."

"Sounds like a niche. Have you heard from Derringer lately?"

"Actually, just yesterday. He said he was going dark into Transnet Archipelago."

"That's a lot of gateway cruising. Well, it must mean he took the job. And I had just thought of something for him. Now I'll have to run into him, how annoying."

"We could pass on a message for you, next time he's in touch."

"No, I can take care of my own. But go ahead and tell him that we talked."

} 85 {

The Lieutenant Corporal stood next to the researcher in the Alpha 1 core, with everything in place to interrupt the Photuris Vortex Anomaly. Statuses incoming.

Lt. Corporal Sorens, Technician Lead, called in over his channels. "Rotating longitudinal arc, torsion 1, four strong, unison report."

"Ghost's Embrace.
Fallen Fledgling.
Overarching Edge.
Bloody Reflection."

"Counter-rotating longitudinal arc, torsion -1, four strong, unison report."

"Family Intention.
Backwards Connection.
Glowing Core.
Heroic Tailspin."

"Buffer Zone 1, Buffer Zone 2, unison report."

"Man At The Bar.
Shadowed Flare."

"Tech Reader, how long till equipment is ready?"

"The passing charge will reach desired level pulse at a quarter hour from now."

"Appropriate, with leeway." Tyson Sorens turned to Arcta Hydraia on his right to meet her eyes and nod. She flickered her notes on the air in front of her and gazed at the room unfocused, hand to her mouth.

"Alpha base 2 reporting." The solid voice of General Ionos, Ehrenson Sorens transmitted to the main line. "We've bundled our frequencies to feed into Buffer Zones 1 and 2 as well as satellites D and E. Ionos base reads and reports. Planetary contingencies are in line. This is the big day."

"Technicians, it's time to compare and align your formulas. Coordinate trajectories with your squadron." The Lt. Cpl. craned his neck around as he listened to pieces of channel chatter, mainly in the direction of various spec prints.

"'Scuse me there's, uh," this rose in volume precedent, "We have an extra ship in formation."

"As do we."

"It just entered our logs officially."

"There are two more of our own ships, not shadows. Both in five strong position."

A visual transmission appeared of Queen Ascendant Charlotte in flight uniform in the technician's seat. "It is my responsibility to be a part of this mission. I have sent record of my full qualifications." The juxtaposed image of General Ionos nodded an extended affirmative to this. "The rudeness of my intrusion requires your tolerant pardon.

"I have also sent you a data point schematic, doubly approved at Loramer, confirming the viability of an extra pair in your formation without any path alteration. This qualified crew, including myself, will now be a part of this maneuver."

The vortex anomaly heaved before Charlotte's gaze. She turned to her pilot and looked back at the massive anomaly. "That looks really complex." Her lips held back bile.

Lieutenant Corporal Sorens stood still as he scanned the new information. He turned slowly toward Ms. Hydraia to find her already facing him.

She gestured to him with her pointer. "We didn't include the last pair because we wanted to minimize the roster - not because of any dynamics issue. We even practiced five strong formation."

"Your Grace, it can be as you wish. From your position you will report to me as Technician Lead."

A message flashed in from the General on Alpha 2. The Lt. Cpl. uttered a small, "Uh oh."

"I've examined the additional crew roster, and I deem it necessary to make a substitution. I will take the place of counter-rotating pilot CR5. The Queen Ascendant and I have flown together before, and I have experience in heroics."

"I find this a comfort," spoke Charlotte from her ship.

Hydraia's posture expressed alarm. "Can we just let a General go pilot one of these?"

Sorens nodded. "They keep fairly current with vehicular training, they won't jump into chairs they can't handle. It happens."

"So he'll just taxi out to the counter-arc? Tech Reader, how long till equipment is at level?"

"It will be another ten minutes. Leeway diminishing but still present."

"So he'll have the time to get out there." Arcta closed her hand into a fist to rest in front of her face.

From Alpha 2, "Sir, Buffer Zone and Ionos Base calls are now routed to you."

"Yes, I am the next person they would want to talk to upon event."

"There is a medical emergency aboard Buffer Zone 2, Shadowed Flare. The signal reader has lost consciousness."

"Get me the pilot's report."

"She was keeping quiet over there until just a minute ago when she blacked out over her controls. I settled her safe in the back, but that leaves me to manage this by myself."

Arcta Hydraia raised both arms widely into the air and brought them down. "Okay before you bring up any qualifications, " she paused in the space between her hands, "I'm a co-inventor of this energy and placement technology. I issued the first ten certifications along with twenty other experts. I'm the best person here, now, to read and understand that position."

Lieutenant Corporal Sorens looked first down at his chest, then up at her, the people around and behind them, then back at the transmission.

"I can do all our coordination from Buffer Zone 2," said Hydraia placatingly. "I might even beat your dad aboard."

"What's your call sign, if you've earned one?"

"Brightening Watcher."

He spoke over transmission. "Okay we're sending in a replacement for Hectic Flare, the unit is now Shadowed

Watcher." Tyson Sorens turned back to her. "Go be the other half." He let her abandon him, and viewed the progress of intermediate craft.

} 86 {

All the action was far from here. Visible - the anomaly couldn't be missed - but the board game and pieces were all obscured. Channel feeds however were a different matter, and these were properly arrayed and attended to by the researcher and her new shipmate. She listened and investigated.

"Arcs move in." Processes were smooth as all the ships attained the velocity to begin acquiring target locations.

At full charge: all set, mirrors setting. Five to a ship, each process individual and coordinated. Their signals were negotiating the anomalous environment.

Flight pairs began lattice switching, to alternately set and boost until every ship's energy charge was placed entirely in connection. In immediate shift, they began altering torsions in a curved net pattern. Light flashed, a mirrortech side effect.

These patterns tightened and new iterations overlaid atop them. Each set of actions felt as though it were sinking in. The signal nature began to generate tensile gravity. The environment was responding.

A collective gear shift enacted the pull, streaming towards the ship boundary around the vortex. Shadow images amid arrows of light swarmed in quantity.

A dragon can hatch a hundred ways. This one, ready to emerge into material was a shared perception - new since its first eight were set to exist in an ages-long otherside trap. They discovered a truth immediately timeless, and encouraged it to be. And in its theoretical existence lay key after key for those that nurtured it. As always, an immeasurable process.

Recently, a dragon advised a human: All you need to do is meddle with it significantly, if you want it to happen according to your symphony. The song of life is ready to play, regardless.

In the quiet world just a gasp was heard in the ear. It was lightning eyes and shadow scales holding everyone in er gaze; the gaze was er grasp. In er grasp there was no pull, only a feeling of envelopment. With an inrushing expansion, all parts of er closed toward every watcher.

And so, a crumbling entropy unfolded, even as something was becoming. And with immediate wisdom, it claimed. The pieces, the wreckage, in wholeness at this moment. To shield, to resist the onrushing for those within its motion was incomprehensible. It was a swift reintegration of life.

This battle was tragic. Arcta's face was frozen like a crying statue as she brought the vessel on its own course away, her new shipmates doubly unconscious next to each other behind.

} 87 {

Arkuda could see the moment reverberating, behaviors and sentences replaying themselves on a fast elliptical, like distance marks on a running track, or the position of a planet during its solar celebration.

Carlos squirmed, sniffling occasionally and rubbing his fists to his eyes. Mireille's hand kept finding various places to rest on her face. Cristobal sat hands curled in his lap, feet even in front of him. Their grandmother's face was a mask.

Arkuda didn't like describing dragon birth to the royal family: Queen and three grandchildren. Reducing its arcane nature into a methodical explanation gave him the shivers, as though 'e would be giving the wrong information; it would not be complete, and would defy definition. This mystery had kept peaceful relations between their people for nearly the entirety of the Imperium's existence. But it was er task to help them understand what had happened in the face of their mother's loss, the woman who was to be the next Queen.

'E addressed the children primarily, as the Queen had bid. "Your mother fell to misdirection, a mistake when confronted with an unknown. We are born of unknowns, that we don't understand when we find them. This one, this dragon, wished to consume on its opening. I'm sorry I couldn't foresee what it was. Now, this one is born, its root existence set. In this way, at this time. We don't know its name yet, so it's still difficult to describe. It has to tell someone what it is."

"We've kept our births a mystery for good reason, because that's what they are, always. Only the first eight of a dragon have some idea of what's going to happen, when or where. They are the only ones who are fairly safe nearby. New dragons have little idea how to control their spatial dimensions at first. It's a unique occurrence every time, and the events are hardly recordable.

"While this one stormed in its birthplace, er first eight appeared around it, which can be typical; in this case it was a shock. I'm saddened by the loss of the entire two-Alpha fleet. Those ancients who appeared are dragons we banished in the War."

Here, the Queen interrupted to explain. "When dragons refer to the War, they mean the one that erupted in the

Imperium during the reign of Oisine, when we had only expanded into the Primatris Federet. It was waged on human planets and over the value of humans' and dragons' rights and lives. The only one since we've known them.

"Those dragons who insisted on their entitlements against humans had the rest working against them, and in a singular work of binding became trapped on the other side of a wall."

Arkuda bowed er head. "We missed our cousins. We felt that their existences were continued, in the persistence of balances. They're not back on friendly terms, clearly. We're going to have to react to defend ourselves. They've dispersed after destroying their vicinity. They are the same Red Nexus of old, minus some. Plus one."

A disheveled driver walked into a bar and took a seat by her favorite bartender. There were a couple occupied booths in the room, but otherwise it was an empty morning. The music was a cheerful rolling ballad at odds with her bereaved look.

"Hot Silver, please."

"You got it. Been a long few weeks, has it? You were here just before Pyrean Midsummer, wasn't it." A smile played across his face as he began to heat and mix.

"Yeah. Actually, I can't think back that far right now. I just watched hundreds of people in uniform ordered to fight something that would kill them. Using means completely unequal to the danger. I had the luxury of my own prerogative, so here I sit." She looked out the window into a ray of sun for a breath while her drink began to steam behind the counter. She looked over doleful, yet matter of fact. "There are dragons at war."

"You don't say." His tone remained light through a furrowed brow. He sprinkled spice over the top and delivered the cup to her hands.

"I wouldn't if I didn't have to." Her head drooped over the cup as she inhaled the steam. Just as she began to close her eyes, someone yelled out from the kitchen.

"Hey Joe! Epic stack, look at this epic stack!"

Joe looked over at his loyal customer. "That's our new dishwasher. He's done it a few times, hasn't broken one yet." He patted the bar as he turned to go to the kitchen.

Looking sideways over her cup, Wendel murmured, "There's a voice..."

Re-emerging, the bartender gestured to her. "You should come see this." Collecting herself, Wendel took a breath and a sip and followed him in.

For a stack, it could be said to be epic. Largest pans and sheets on the bottom, going to smaller pans, to platters and appropriately-sized dishes with the occasional balancing item, to a rotating tower of mugs and cups that ended in a pyramid. Other words that came to mind were magnificent; unprecarious; commendable.

She looked over to appraise the stacker and was greeted with a smiling face. "It's you," said the boy, grinning with his mouth open.

She blinked at Toller, suddenly breathless. "Hey, it's... it's you too." She gravitated toward him to hold him in her arms for a moment. "You got a job, I see?"

The boy poked Joe in the side. "I left the capital after the Aquari concert. That really capped off the whole experience for me. At the docks, I found a ship with room headed for Dalmeera, so." He pointed to the stack of dishes.

Wendel turned to the bartender. "Joe I hate to tell you this, but your dishwasher is overqualified."

He laughed. "Yeah, I know. I just figured I could get away with it for a little while."

"Well, you're good at doing it." She smiled at the both of them and looked at the cup in her hand, still steaming. She looked back up at the boy. "Hey have you tried this stuff?"

Toller looked at Joe. "Well I'm not really old enough, no."

Wendel tilted her head at the bartender. "Is he old enough?"

Joe eyed the stack of dishes, all clean. "He's older than I was. He can have his own cup. Stay back here. And would you take that apart and put it away?" The last he said to Toller, who saluted.

Toller set a chair on the countertop beside it, showing how unprecarious the stack really was. He climbed on top and began filling his arms with the assorted dishware. "You didn't take long to come back, either."

She made a long sniff. "It all really depends." She just watched him do his job. "So you remembered the place?"

"Actually I met Joe at the seadocks where they were bringing up shellfish. He seemed like someone I could hustle for work, and I was right. Man was carrying too much." He laughed and laughed with the dishes. "He brought me back here and I knew where I was."

Halfway down the stack, the bartender returned with one for the boy and one for him. The three clinked mugs and held them together for a moment, looking at the pictures in steam and spice and silver.

Upon his first sip, Toller made a face like he just saw a beast. Then he looked into the cup. "Are you kidding me, what is this?"

Joe savored his sip and lifted his head. "Just something good we make here."

Wendel smacked her lips in agreement and ran her tongue over her teeth. "Well young one, I want to tell you. You've got options."

"Oh, really?"

"Yeah, really. With me, for one."

"I could be mad at you." Joe wiggled his mug in the air.

Wendel took a long, appreciative sip. "And lose your favorite customer?"

Re-Issue Changes

From the previous version titled
"Fire On All Sides" to this
version, now "Fire Within", a few
changes have been made.

Mainly:
- Draconid Agender Pronouns
- certain character title uses
- contents section titles fully
aligned to contained two-word
phrases
- choice turns of phrase
- volume title

Story events haven't been
changed, and details have not
been removed.

grammatical notes

~ Draconid Singular Agendered Pronouns: 'e/er/emself

'E was wondering to emself as 'e went back to er car. Once 'e joined them, they all took themselves on an adventure.

This set of singular pronouns was given to me by Bogi Takacs, and I have been told they have a history of use going back to the 1920's. I found them natural to pronounce, and sufficient for indicating individuals amongst a group, on the written page.

~ "Alright" and "All Right" are both valid usages with slightly different connotations. The previous disambiguates the expression from the meaning of correctness, toward that of a generally positive value. Mark Twain & James Joyce agree with me, on the record.

~ Lays down to rest. Lies only regarding untruths.
Every thing and every being can gracefully lay down, lay upon, be laid alongside, and lay amongst, with no confusion or trouble, as comfortably as one might lay beside a natural river. Lying so often means something else, and in writing, which has fewer contextual guides, I'd rather be clear as to when I'm doing it. Used as such in Bones of Starlight.

SOLDIER DIDN'T LIE… DOWN, SLAIN NEXT WHILE PONDERING POSSIBLE MEANINGS OF DECEASED OFFICER'S INTERRUPTED COMMAND
If Only Officer Had Used Lay Parlance
[…which can also mean something else, but war is full of lies, making confusion more likely…]

continued overleaf >

~ Tense-shifting.
In this series, a tense-shift denotes a variation from third-person narrative.
Sometimes: thoughts and dreams in 1st-person-present tense with no
other separating marks, sometimes in their own paragraph/chapter.

~ the invisible-em dash - or, em is for emodern
Andrea Stewart lamented the fading of ye olde em dash--this jointed,
club-ended and broken entity, visually chaining words while indicating a
suspended relative pause between phrases. Many now favor the 'invisible
em' - causally, it fools foolish computer-age word processors seeking to
meddle, but effectively also visually demonstrates suspensefully-linked
phrases. "I favor it, and use ye olde em for--" and here she paused
while quoting herself, "--linked statements fragmented by pausing a
quote." Distinguished by, well - space itself, from the en-dash which links
individual words into a united phrase.

~ Self-tuning rules of grammar as one might self-tune a guitar.
A guitar tuned to itself can play a song. A book - particularly a one-
author book dealing with an alternate universe - can (with consistency)
internally re-determine a guideline or two, without harming what other
books do on their pages.

"Its better to be wrong than be pendant." - Margaret Kiljoy, saying no to
grammar nazis

yours in earnest,
eva l. elasigue

THANKS

TO MY FRIDAY HARBOR ISLAND FAMILY - YOU GET
ME

MY DEAR RELATIVES NEAR AND FAR, FOR CARING

MY DOG, SPIRIT, FOR KEEPING HOME
& ALL MY ANIMAL AND PLANT FRIENDS,
NICE TO KNOW YOU

TO MY CONVENTION COMMUNITY FOR HELPING ME
GROW

TO MY FESTIVAL FAMILIES FOR KEEPING ME
GROUNDED

TO MY CREATIVE KARASS FOR ALL THE GREAT &
MAGNIFICENT WORK

THE REVOLUTIONARIES WHO'VE INSPIRED ME AND
GIVEN ME STRENGTH & POSSIBILITY

THE INSTITUTIONS & ESTABLISHMENTS THAT
OPENED THEIR DOORS TO WORK WITH ME

TO STRANGERS WITH OPEN HEARTS

FOR FRIENDS WHO'VE KEPT FAITH WITH ME

HERE'S TO US

NEXT

BONES OF STARLIGHT 1:
FIRE WITHIN
IN CLASSIC POCKETBOOK PAPERBACK

BONES OF STARLIGHT 2:
ABYSS SURROUNDING

BONES OF STARLIGHT 3:
GREATER BEYOND

KEEP IN TOUCH
BONESOFSTARLIGHT.COM
EVALISAELASIGUE.WORDPRESS.COM

FACEBOOK: EVA L. ELASIGUE
INSTAGRAM: PRIMAL . SPIRAL
TWITTER: @PRIMALSPIRAL

about the author

Eva L. Elasigue combines an honor-awarded imagination
with scientific & empirical backgrounds to create the fantasy
space opera trilogy Bones of Starlight, as well as works from
poetic to humorous for internet and stage. She lives with
her dog Spirit, on San Juan Island, Washington State US, in
the Pacific Northwest Cascadia bioregion. She is currently
continuing her debut series and manages Primal Spiral, an
imprint/events collective/studio. A mixed-media artist and
renaissance woman, she loves music and the wilderness.

COLOPHON

Baskerville
)Bodoni Ornaments(

special thanks to gLuk:
WabRoYe
ResamitzSO1
SPINWERADC